Meet the Wife

Clive Sinclair

Meet the Wife

PICADOR

First published 2002 by Picador
an imprint of Pan Macmillan Ltd
Pan Macmillan, 20 New Wharf Road, London N1 9RR
Basingstoke and Oxford
Associated companies throughout the world
www.panmacmillan.com

ISBN 0 330 34841 8

1 3 5 7 9 8 6 4 2

A CIP catalogue record for this book is available from
the British Library.

Typeset by Intype London Ltd
Printed and bound in Great Britain by
Mackays of Chatham plc, Chatham, Kent

Acknowledgements

The author is glad to acknowledge a grant from the Authors' Foundation. He also wishes to thank a handful of early readers: Yosl and Audrey Bergner, Pamela and Jonathan Lubell, Murray and Sheila Baumgarten, Cecil Helman, and – first among equals – Haidee Becker.

For Seth, Thomas, and James

CONTENTS

Meet the Wife

The Naked and the Dead

Meet the Wife

What the past and the future have in common is our imagination which conjures them. And our imagination is rooted in our eschatological dread: the dread of thinking that we are without precedence or consequence. The stronger that dread, the more detailed our notion of antiquity or utopia.

Joseph Brodsky

I enter the Hotel Aubergine with the aplomb of a man in possession of a big secret. Keen to cock a snook at my rivals I look around for familiar faces, only to have my eye arrested by an outlandish presence: a much-tossed sea-dog. How can I be so confident that this human anachronism is more accustomed to having the Med beneath his feet than terra firma? In a word: experience. My profession has taught me to judge people at a glance. The man's leathery complexion speaks of force nine gales, his piercing gaze of far horizons. He could equally be a ski instructor, I suppose, but we happen to be on the coast, not in the mountains. Observing those azure eyes more closely I perceive that they are wet. Then I note with growing alarm that tears are flowing down his careworn cheeks, and soaking the roots of his russet whiskers. They are the unambiguous heralds of bad news; they announce that the Marshal has breathed his last. Too soon, too soon.

Overwhelmed with anguish I hug the lachrymose mariner. 'Your grief is a microcosm of our nation's sorrow,' I mumble, now sobbing myself.

The man's companion – his own son, I presume – looks at me as if I were a madman. 'Do we know you, good sir?' he asks.

'Not personally,' I reply, 'but your loss is also my loss.'

'Then I presume that you knew my beloved mother from old,' he replies. 'For it is her that we mourn.'

Decency forces me to stifle a cheer. 'So the great helmsman still lives?' I gasp, giving the old salt's rough-clad shoulder a squeeze.

'Don't worry,' he rumbles, 'that undeserving son of a bitch soldiers on, while my faithful wife has long since been reduced to ash.'

I can restrain myself no longer. 'The gods be praised,' I cry, 'I am not too late!' Let them regard me with distaste. What do I care? The scoop that will make me the most famous and the most envied journalist in the literate world is still on the cards.

•

Scoop? Forget it. I am too canny a pro to spill the beans prematurely, but I am prepared to let you in on another trade secret. I am dying for a pee. I may be crossing the lobby with the insouciance of a dromedary, but in truth my bladder is one drop short of bursting. As it happens, I have been travelling for twelve hours and haven't had a jimmy riddle since leaving my apartment in the capital to catch the dawn flight to old Endive, on our farthest shore. I attempted to break my duck on the aeroplane, but did nothing more than stand above the stainless steel bowl with a bone-dry dick. Nor was I able to perform upon landing, having been discomforted by the presence of two noisy juveniles and their father in the airport's unhygienic urinal.

The problem is an old one, whose remote origins must lie in the lavatories of my infancy. I was an only child, but even so was not spared sibling rivalry. My father had a pet piglet, which he treated better than his son. They went everywhere together, the piglet trotting at his side like a dog. But when I tried to befriend it, the bloody thing wet itself in my lap, making it look as though I were the incontinent one (indeed, I was punished as such). Whatever the cause, the sphincter designed to prevent such accidents has become a pocket dictator, censoring my freedom of action and movement. I am hardly a political dissident, but my life is a continuous rebellion against that little muscle, otherwise I would never leave the safety of my own water closet.

Thanks to my easy charm the receptionist remains

unaware of my desperate need and records the details of my identity card with agonizing exactitude.

'You are the fifteenth journalist to register in the last two days,' she remarks. 'Is there a convention or something?'

'There's certainly something,' I reply mysteriously.

Obviously she is not privy to the rumours of the Marshal's imminent demise. Unlike Gumbo of the *Word*, Chickpea of the *Witness*, and Haricot of the *Truth*, all of whom are playing a rumbustious game of blackjack practically under my nose. Other dog-eat-dog hacks hog the scattered armchairs, drinking high-octane slivovitz while they wait for the dismal announcement from the Marshal's private island. What else can they do in an out-of-season seaside resort? The more enterprising have brought seductive sidekicks along to alleviate the boredom. Gumbo goes bust and, glancing up, spots me.

'Why, look who's here,' he says, 'it's the Court Circular.'

Chickpea and Haricot chortle. They call me the Court Circular because they think I am porky – which I deny, though I'd admit to portly – and a sycophant – a charge I reject categorically.

'One of these days you'll laugh on the other side of your faces,' I snap, 'mark my words.'

'We're shaking in our boots,' cries Gumbo, while the other two just hoot.

'Here is your key,' says the receptionist. 'Room 352, on the third floor. Enjoy your stay.' But I am already on the way to relieve Mafeking.

Alone in my *en suite* bathroom I fully open the faucets, hoping that the sound will have the desired effect upon my sphincter, and blissfully empty my bladder in thick spurts. Drained, I return to the bedroom only to discover that the place is swarming with the local species of cockroach, shiny dark creatures that dart around like iron filings. I am more powerful, but they are fleeter and more numerous. Annihilating them is an exhausting business. Eventually I offer terms. Why not? They are pleasanter company than my contemporaries downstairs. The treaty holds: I refrain from killing them, and they do not disturb my slumber. Nor, alas, does the telephone with news of the elusive scoop. I awaken naturally and pray that the Marshal survives the day. After a breakfast of salami and eggs I inform the receptionist that I am going for a stroll on the beach, and give her strict instructions to page me should my presence be required by a higher authority.

The old town – formerly the habitat of seafarers, now a harbour for the world-weary – stands on the beak of a perpendicular cliff overlooking the endless sea. Beyond the horizon lies Paprika, home of the ruddy-haired pirates who once raided these shores in search of indigenous beauties to stock their local

seraglios. The characteristic architecture suggests that
many of these bold corsairs themselves became the
slaves of love and dropped anchor hereabouts.
Anyway, the town grew vertically. Its narrow streets,
squeezed between unbroken rows of venerable sky-
scrapers, are more like canyons. It is a place that keeps
you in the dark, both literally and metaphorically.

Passing beneath an ancient archway decorated with
a mystifying rebus, I step on to a small belvedere.
Directly below is the golden bow of the beach. At its
eastern tip is a high-vaulted cave, once filled with fine
statuary collected by the Emperor Tiberius. One of his
palaces was adjacent; now it's reduced to its foun-
dations, a three-dimensional blueprint in the sand.
Ancient historians tell of an ill-starred meal served in
the very mouth of the cave. It seems that while Tiberius and guests were tucking into larks' tongues or
whatever, a massive rockfall crushed several servants
and caused widespread panic. Tiberius was saved only
because his aide, two-faced Sejanus, covered his
Emperor's body with his own. I like to think I would
do no less for the Marshal.

The villa was abandoned thereafter and the cave
remained undisturbed for nearly two millennia until
a new road was built along the coast. The contractors
(not unreasonably) decided that the deserted cavern
would be a useful repository for their equipment, and
thus rediscovered the statues that graced the place in

its glory days. The problem was that they had been reduced to 15,000 fragments. The authorities prepared to transport them to the capital for restoration, but the locals, suspecting that their unexpected legacy would never return, blockaded the road. As a result the sculptures – repaired where possible – are once again visible *in situ*. The dominant pieces, both in quality and size, illustrate episodes from the *Odyssey*; most notably the blinding of Polyphemus (who is considerably larger than life in all departments, and easily apparent from where I stand).

At the western end of the beach is the new marina. Within its breakwaters I can clearly see the blue-riband cruiser commissioned by the Marshal to ferry him from the mainland to his island retreat. The beach, to my surprise, is all but deserted, there being but two souls on the entire strand. Completing my descent I am able to identify them as yesterday's tearful captain and his cabin boy. The lad is throwing a stick for a muscular little hound to chase. It is an exceedingly repetitious game: the dog retrieves the stick for the umpteenth time – either from the sand, or from the surf – and drops it at the boy's feet, whereupon the boy raises it aloft and tosses it yet again. Meanwhile the older man keeps his eye trained upon the distant conjunction of sea and sky, as if expecting Barbarossa and his crew to show at any moment.

The sand is soft and I leave deep impressions as I

march towards the sea. The boy, I note, has introduced a variation into the game. He holds the stick at head height and the dog leaps towards it with such energy that it rises more than twice its own length above the ground. Its stamina seems inexhaustible; up and down it goes, apparently attached to the branch with elastic. Progress becomes less laboured when I reach the firmer sand, still wet from the morning tide. In passing I acknowledge the other beneficiaries of the ozone and the autumnal sun. Only the dog pays any attention. It runs to greet me, as if I were its long-lost master returned home from a distant war or some other bloody escapade. I wave it away, but this gesture only serves to excite it the more. Using its forepaws as twin shovels, it begins to burrow in the sand at my feet. Such is its manic determination that a deep hole appears within moments.

'If he keeps this up he'll be in China before the week is out,' I say to the boy, who is watching the super-canine performance with equal incredulity.

'Did you bury something there?' he enquires suspiciously.

'Of course not,' I reply.

Suddenly the dog loses interest in the original excavation and begins to tunnel elsewhere.

'Look,' cries the boy, 'he's trying to catch the reflection from your watch glass.'

Sure enough the mutt is worrying the sand precisely where the shiny crescent dances.

'The boy's right,' I cry, *'c'est un chien* in search of *temps perdu.'*

The boy looks at me as if his first impression has been triumphantly confirmed. 'Which one of us is not?' murmurs his father, finally breaking his silence.

'You must have expected to find a hotel as empty as this beach,' I say. 'Instead it is swarming with unsavoury types: reporters more interested in the intimate parts of their feather-brained secretaries than the impending apocalypse. I am the exception. You too are not of that ilk. May I be so bold as to enquire what you are doing in Endive at this unseasonable time?'

Before he has a chance to open his mouth our newly forged bond is shattered by a superannuated bellhop, who is staggering across the sand like a hobbled Hermes while calling me by name.

Nodding at the father and son I go to meet him, accompanied by the dog, still bent upon pursuing its impossible quest.

'You must proceed directly to the harbour and board the Marshal's yacht,' gasps the veteran, shoving me in the right direction.

'Hold your horses,' I say. 'I can't go to the island without my tape recorder, and that's still in my hotel room.'

'Not any more,' says the bellhop, handing it to me with a contemptuous sneer.

For the sake of my good name I should mention that I did not leave the tape recorder in my room by accident, but so as to have an excuse to return and *en passant* snatch a quick wee in private. Now I am fated to be ballasted with a full bladder. Reaching the marina in record time, I pause at a kiosk to phone my editor in the capital. 'Hold the front page!' I cry.

Having tipped my guide I cross the gangplank and board the Marshal's yacht. Its captain greets me formally. I am not a prepossessing figure at the best of times, and I can tell from his expression that he is wondering why someone like me – neither a doctor nor a politico – should be granted such privileged access. Perhaps he puts me down as a mortician. It is a fair question. Why should I (of all people) have been granted the singular honour of a deathbed interview with the Marshal? There, the cat is out of the bag! After all I am a man of very modest achievements, neither famous nor powerful; a man who has simply done his best for his country, and his newspaper. In short, a simple patriot; loyal and straight.

As we leave the security of the harbour's horseshoe I look back at the beach – where the boy is still throwing the stick for the hound to chase – and the cliff-top town, which seems as impregnable as a walled fortress. Ahead of us lies the blessed isle itself, whose

the marina my obit would still have been too late to make the final edition.

'What a time to take a fishing trip,' says Gumbo, with a smirk.

'Catch anything big?' ask Chickpea and Haricot maliciously.

They insist upon listening while I telephone my editor. He is not in a forgiving mood.

'Every paper in Capsicum has a special issue on the streets telling the world that an era has ended,' he bellows, with sufficient gusto that all around can hear. 'Every paper, bar one. I've got them on my desk in front of me. The *Word* somehow knows that the Marshal embraced his end with serenity, being completely free of personal concerns. His only thoughts, it seems, were for the future of the Federation.' Gumbo takes a bow. 'The *Witness* goes one better, printing extracts from his medical records,' continues my editor, 'while the *Truth* has even got hold of his last words. "My hand is falling from the tiller," he is supposed to have said. "Be sure that a strong one replaces it." ' Chickpea and Haricot embrace one another. 'And what of us?' concludes my editor ominously. 'The Marshal's death seems to have escaped our ace reporter's attention entirely. As a consequence our final edition proudly promises an exclusive interview with him on the morrow. Unless you can deliver the goods, don't ever show your ugly face in this building again. Do you understand what I'm saying?'

'Oh dear, oh dear', says Gumbo.

Standing before my jeering contemporaries I feel like a schoolboy; the little schoolboy who, unable to use the kindergarten's alfresco latrine, one day was forced by his increasingly unpredictable sphincter to wet himself in fits and starts until his shame was visible to all. I wanted the ground to swallow me then, and I wish it would swallow me now. So complete is my mortification.

At such moments of crisis a man needs his mother. How I long to hear her call me, 'My darling boy.' But I dare not telephone her, for fear that my voice will betray my humiliation. The last thing I want is to cause her any disquiet. She was so proud when her only son became a reporter on a national newspaper. As far as she is concerned, that is what I shall remain. Mother is equally protective. When her cancer was diagnosed she did her best to keep the dire news from me. Went so far as to refuse chemotherapy, lest her hair fall out and give the game away. It was her sister who enlightened me. Between us we persuaded her to heed the experts. She's on the mend now, or so she tells me. Having no other source of solace, I retire to my room and curl up like a foetus in my bug-infested bed.

I awaken ravenous from a fretful slumber and

decide to eat breakfast, since it is already paid for. I hasten to the dining room, only to find myself at the tail end of a mass exodus.

'What's the hurry?' I ask a photographer, who's taking advantage of the lull to stuff his numerous pockets with croissants and *pains au chocolat*.

'There's a report – still unconfirmed – of shooting at the late Marshal's country seat,' he replies. 'It's got everyone in a tizz.'

'Which country seat would that be?' I ask.

'Pomodoro,' he replies.

A mere twenty-five miles to the east! Maybe I can redeem myself yet. I exit through the revolving door and stumble into chaos: two dozen journalists and no taxis. I can hear Gumbo crying, 'What are we waiting for?' *'Avanti! Avanti!'* echo Chickpea and Haricot, trying to push themselves to the front of the line. Once there Gumbo accosts a hapless porter.

'My good man,' he says imperiously, 'we require transport immediately.'

'How big is your party?' asks the porter.

'Three,' says Gumbo.

'Four,' I interject.

'Who invited the Court Circular?' ask Chickpea and Haricot.

'Three, four, it makes no difference,' says the porter. 'Either way you won't get a taxi for at least two hours.'

Looking at Gumbo's furrowed brow and clenched fists I fear for the fellow's life.

While the exclusive trio discusses what tactics to adopt, I notice the matelot and his offspring opening the doors of an all-terrain Zatopec (presumably hired for the duration of their stay). Since my companions aren't keen on my company, I neglect to mention the fact and silently remove myself from their presence.

'Are you going east?' I ask the sailor's boy (who is in the driving seat).

'Yes,' replies the lad.

'In that case,' I say, 'may I have a lift?'

'I've no objections,' says the sailor indifferently.

Gliding past, I wave to Gumbo and his chums from the comfort of my leatherette seat, an almost imperceptible gesture copied from the Queen of Hearts herself. It has the desired effect.

'Where are you going?' asks the youthful driver.

'Pomodoro,' I reply.

'There's a coincidence,' says the seafarer.

'You should be warned,' I say. 'It might be dangerous.'

'Dangerous? Forgive me, sir,' laughs the sailor, 'but you look the kind of man who would faint if pricked by a rose.'

Shadows of umbrella pines lie across the straight road like sleepers, giving it the appearance of a railway track. The optical illusion lends our short journey gravitas; Pomodoro becomes our station, our destination, our destiny. It was gifted to the first Duke of Pimento in the year dot. He immediately constructed a palatial villa on the land and a square tower, both of which still stand. However, the town built by his retainers was not so sturdy; by the sixteenth century all its dwellings and churches were in ruins. But the Dukes of Pimento were obstinate fellows, and they remained *in situ* until ousted by twentieth-century revolutionaries. At that time Pomodoro's chief glory was its garden, laid out by the last Duchess in the 1930s and said to be no less beautiful than the Elysian Fields. She felt that the medieval ruins (while certainly picturesque) lacked vitality, so she planted them with vegetable life. Thanks to her vision, mulberry trees now grow in unroofed halls and wisteria clings to broken church walls, while golden carp adorn the crystal rivulets. The Duchess was quickly replaced as the *genius loci* by the Marshal's first wife, whose fingers were also green.

As soon as we pass through its unguarded gates a breezy swirl of reds, yellows, russets, and other shades from the autumnal palette waltzes away with our senses. Before we have a chance to regain them we are knocked sideways by a ravishing perfume; one that speaks of maturity (the fleshy promise of ripeness), and passion (the smouldering bite of burning juniper). Within moments we spy the smoking bonfires and the fruits themselves. Vines running wild, overburdened with great bunches of purple grapes, groves of darkening figs, and orchards ablaze with glowing nectarines. It takes a conscious effort not to follow the example of the intoxicated wasps, desperately feeding their addiction at the expense of the pears. This frenzy of the senses is further fed by the piercing thrill of birdsong. At any moment I expect to see Bacchus dart from behind a sweet chestnut. Fortunately our bucolic madness is suddenly soothed by the sound of sweet water bubbling up from a quartet of hidden springs.

We leave the car beside the quattrocento villa and knock upon its gigantic wooden doors.

'You never told me what you were doing in Endive,' I say to the sailor. 'May I now ask the purpose of your visit to Pomodoro?'

Again his reply is porlocked by the entry of a minor character, this time an octogenarian butler. Having opened the portals the stooped relic of the *ancien régime* admits us immediately, so glad of company that he neglects all his duties, not even asking us our business. He leads us into the great hall, now empty save for a grand piano.

'They cleaned the place out,' he gasps, 'took everything except me.' While the butler stands in silent contemplation, the boy begins to pick out a hornpipe on the venerable instrument. 'Take it easy, young man,' cautions the butler, 'that piano was once the property of the immortal Liszt. Nor was he the only musician of genius to visit Pomodoro. Once the old Duke – the last Duke's father – grabbed my sleeve when I was passing with a tray of lemonade and muttered, "Funny little man, Brahms. Used to smoke a cigar before breakfast." A remarkable event in itself, since he had never addressed me directly before, let alone made physical contact. Where have they all gone? Why have they left me behind?'

He meanders down a flight of steps into a vast brick-lined cellar. We follow uncertainly. Along the length of its walls run slatted shelves, upon which stands a decaying army of apples and pears. We march to the end like visiting generals inspecting the troops.

'Tell me,' says the butler, 'what am I to do with this cornucopia now that there is no one left to enjoy any of it?' He turns and opens a small door which allows access to a vast lawn. 'All you parvenus can see is the material world,' says the butler, 'but I see what is no longer visible. I see tables covered with snow-white cloths, dozens of distinguished guests, and an equal number of servants offering afternoon tea. In its heyday Pomodoro attracted beauties from right across Europa. Some even came from the other side of the globe. They rolled up in their open cars with their latest beaux and their repulsive chihuahuas. Nothing much changed after the Marshal took over. Except the quality of the guests. Can you gentlemen explain why women of influence are always uglier after revolutions?'

As we stroll aimlessly across the grass a supersonic bee suddenly passes close to my ear. The sailor identifies the threat at once.

'Get down,' he cries, flattening his son.

I follow suit, but the ancient butler seems blind to the danger. Far from ducking, he zigzags slowly over the lawn as if taking last orders from the merry tables he alone can see. We plead with him to remove himself from the line of fire, to give priority to his immediate needs for once. To no avail. A sniper's bullet pierces his chest. He falls to his knees, gasps, 'My master calls me, I must not say no,' and dies.

'Can you see where the murderous cowards are skulking?' I ask the sailor.

'Look to the heights beyond the estate,' he advises. 'See how they are honeycombed with caves. I can guarantee that each of those accursed cavities will contain at least one resident assassin.'

Sure enough I spot numerous shadowy figures, made more visible by the incongruous presence of monocles, tiny moons that catch the antemeridian sun. These make them look like gents of the old school, except that the monocles are actually telescopic sights and they are more probably uncouth irregulars from the other side of the mountains. Those mountains are one of the numerous fault lines in the Federation,

hitherto stabilized by the Marshal's indomitable personality. Without him the tectonic plates have
obviously begun to shift with unforeseen rapidity.

'We are in mortal peril,' notes the sailor, as bullets
continue to dimple the grass. 'They already have us
pinned down. When they get bored with their sport
they'll have no difficulty in picking us off, one by one.'

Just my luck! I have witnessed the first victim
fall; the first victim of the cataclysm, the first victim of
the next civil war. In other words, I have probably
redeemed my career with a world exclusive. One that
I am not going to live long enough to write. Even so I
curse myself for not asking the butler's name. As the
bullets continue to fly, it occurs to me that I don't
know the identity of my doomed companions either.
But I am certainly familiar with the woman who has
suddenly appeared beside me.

'For heaven's sake, Mother,' I scream, 'take cover
immediately or you'll end up like the butler.'

'They'll be doing me a favour,' she says bitterly. 'Do
not be alarmed, my darling boy, but you are not the
only one with an unpleasant secret. Your mother is as
sick as our poor country. The blow came out of the
blue last month, when my doctor began to suspect
that the cancer had returned. He begged me to have
exploratory surgery. Naturally I put it off as long as
possible so as not to worry you. But now I am in such
pain that I have no choice. Do not worry, I shall not

distress you with a detailed description of my infirm-
ities, or the indignities they are about to visit upon
me. Boys should be thinking about their futures, not
their sick mamas.'

'Mother, do not torture me with such nonsense,' I
cry, 'please just lie down. You won't be safe, but you'll
be safer.'

'Fear has unseated our friend's reason,' says the
youth to his father. 'See how he addresses thin air.'

'My son the materialist,' scoffs the sailor. 'The ill-
omened butler was quite correct; there is always more
than one reality. As far as I am concerned this dainty
lawn is the rough surf. Yonder mountains are mighty
cliffs. And those bastards trying to annihilate us are
the one-eyed followers of Polyphemus, King of the
Cyclops.'

'Tell me again how you killed him, Father,' demands
the young man.

The older obliges. 'First I got the old devil drunk,'
he says. 'Then I put out his one eye with a wooden
shaft, hardened in the fire. Finally I fled, disguised as
a ram. If only I could get back to those caves, I'd tear
every one of those gangsters apart with my bare hands.'

The only question is which of us is the bigger
lunatic: the one who is conversing with an otherwise
invisible mother, or the one who thinks he's Odysseus?

We are saved in the end by the sudden arrival of
Gumbo, Chickpea, and Haricot, who unwittingly lead

a jeremiad of journalists into the valley of death. The gunmen, tempted by the greater number, redirect their fire, granting us a stay of execution.

'Run for your life!' screams the seaman, leaping to his feet and bounding over the grass hand in hand with his son.

I follow, *sans* mama, and dive headlong into the cellar. Seeing our desperate flight my peers hesitate, until a bullet grazes Chickpea's forehead. Thus prompted they too turn tail, shedding notebooks, tape recorders, and even cameras in a mad scramble for shelter. Their undignified retreat looks so farcical I cannot help but laugh.

'Believe me,' says the mock Odysseus, 'you were no Fred Astaire.'

We retrace our steps through the deserted mansion and regain the Zatopec.

'If such things can happen at Pomodoro in a supposedly pacific era,' says the ancient mariner to his apprentice, 'you can imagine what it was like in my day, when anarchy defied the gods, and perhaps begin to appreciate why the journey home took so bloody long.'

By way of contrast, the drive back to the Hotel Aubergine is entirely without incident. I congratulate the young driver upon his composure; both under fire, and (subsequently) at the wheel.

'I know you think I'm bonkers,' I say, as I turn to

go, 'but I bet I've still got enough marbles to guess your name.'

'I doubt it,' he says indifferently.

'Is it Rumpelstiltskin?' I ask.

He laughs. 'Not even warm,' he says.

'Is it Asparagus Rex?' I ask.

'You're in Antarctica,' he replies.

'I don't suppose it's Telemachus?' I enquire.

He looks at me in amazement. 'How did you know that?' he gasps.

'One of the benefits of a classical education,' I reply.

Back in the Hotel Aubergine I quickly discover that my derring-do has been an empty gesture. It seems that while I was dodging the bullets of those hot-headed troglodytes, their equivalents on this side of the mountain were busy cutting the telephone lines to Capsicum. The operator assures me that all connections are consequently impossible, irrespective of their urgency. I beg her to keep trying. Her stubborn refusal to assist me verges on the hostile. I am in Endive, but I might as well be on Mars. My editor is out of reach. Nor can I ascertain the precise whereabouts of my mother, let alone the real state of her health. At which point I am accosted by a morose foreigner. The presence of an expensive camera suggests that he is a photojournalist.

'Can you tell me what the hell is going on?' he pleads (in a voice that marks him as a native of distant

Buffalo). 'I came to photograph the unique fauna of your coastal forests. Instead I find myself revisiting the Wild West.'

I push the fellow aside and retreat to my room, stricken with unassuaged anxiety. My suspense is mercifully short-lived, for I find the object of my concern sitting on the edge of my bed. Her face is white, and her hands (which are pressed deep into the quilt) are swarming with the indigenous cockroaches.

'Mother, they'll eat you to the bone,' I cry. 'Kill them, for heaven's sake!'

'What right do I have to harm them?' she replies. 'In the eyes of the world they are our moral superiors.'

'Why say such a terrible thing?' I demand.

'Because it is the simple truth,' she replies. 'Even before the Marshal's body was cold his own guards began to loot the island stronghold. They set free the lions, tigers, and other carnivorous *Felidae* their master kept in his private zoo. Of course the beasts immediately turned upon one another and began to fight to the death for the same piece of ground. The citizens of Ancho were no less ferocious. As soon as they heard the news they slaughtered as many of our people as they could find, not excepting those who had lived in their province for generations. The federal government in Capsicum, rightly regarding these pogroms as an act of secession, immediately dispatched troops to crush the revolt. This is what the world saw, and uses in evidence against us.'

'How could such a disaster happen so quickly?' I cry. 'Did no one see it coming?'

'We all did,' replies Mother, 'and we said nothing. That is our sin.'

'But I didn't,' I moan. 'What kind of journalist does that make me?'

'My poor boy,' she says. 'You have lived your entire life in a totalitarian society dedicated to the suffocation of the individual. The only way to thrive in such an environment is to lie, or to blind yourself to the truth. I know you did it with the best of intentions; to make your mother proud. That too is my failure.'

'Are you implying that the Marshal was not a great man?' I ask, deeply shocked.

'Strong, certainly; great, definitely not,' she replies. 'He had the strength to keep the lions and tigers locked up. But he lacked the greatness to teach them to live together.'

'What will become of us?' I say.

'I don't know, my darling boy,' she replies, 'but I do know that you have been stranded on the wrong side of the border, that you are trapped in what has become enemy territory. I long to hold you in my arms once more, but I fear for your safety should you attempt to return. If you are not killed by the Anchovies, you may be shot by our own side in error, as you nearly were this morning. I repeat, do not risk your life on my account.'

With that warning my mother vanishes, leaving nothing behind but two valleys filled with cock-roaches, and the slight aroma of talc.

As the hours pass my misery becomes so pronounced that I prefer to seek out the company of Gumbo and his ilk rather than remain alone in my room. But where are they? The lobby is empty, and the only keys missing from the rack behind the recep-tionist are my own and those belonging to the legendary seafarer and his son. My first apprehension is that they are all hot on the trail of another massive story that only I will fail to report; another negative scoop, as it were. But then I begin to worry for their safety; perhaps they made a dash for the frontier and were gunned down by trigger-happy guards. Or perhaps they never got that far and were massacred *en route* by a band of bloodthirsty Anchovies. As it happens the border-guards did open fire upon their charabanc, puncturing its front wheels. However, they were ignored by the Anchovies (who mistook them for their own), thanks to the fact that their vehicle was hired from the biggest travel agent in Endive.

Chickpea is the first to enter the hotel, a bloodied bandage wrapped around his forehead. For once he seems genuinely pleased to see me.

'It's the Court Circular,' he informs his companions, 'and he's in one piece.'

Then he trots towards me, arms outstretched.

'I owe you my life,' he gasps, embracing me like a brother. 'If your famous sprint across the grass hadn't caused me to step back in astonishment I'd now have JFK's head on my shoulders, for sure.'

'That's no less than the truth,' says Haricot. 'You definitely saved his bacon.'

'We'd be honoured if you'd join us for a much needed beer,' adds Gumbo.

Overwhelmed by their *bonhomie*, I follow them into the bar. '*Garçon*,' demands Gumbo, 'bring us four cold Talibans, and a large bowl of olives.'

'What shall we drink to?' asks Haricot, when the beers are delivered.

'A peaceful future?' I suggest.

'I've a better idea,' says Chickpea, raising his glass. 'To the Four Musketeers: to Haricot, Gumbo, Chickpea, and . . . hey, what's your real name?'

'Pumpkin,' I say.

'And Pumpkin,' he echoes.

We touch glasses and drink deeply. 'Mmm,' says Haricot, 'nice and yeasty.'

The room is warm, the beer icy, causing my glass to break out in a cold sweat. I watch as baubles of condensation descend its bulbous flanks like tears down a fat man's chops. It seems that even inanimate

objects are beginning to mourn for the Federation, the
Federation that was. Then I notice that my own eyes
are overflowing, that my own cheeks are damp, and I
realize that I am experiencing the spontaneous emis-
sion of bodily fluid; but these are not tears of sorrow.

On the contrary. Sorrow has brought forth sweetness: for the first time in my life I have been accepted
into a group.

After the initial outburst of enthusiasm we fall silent
and chew contemplatively on the peppery green olives.

'My friends,' I say, looking from one to the other,
'I'm suddenly in quite a pickle. You could even call it
an identity crisis. For as long as I can remember the
Marshal was my idol. In other words, I now concede
that the sobriquet you gave me was well merited.
But that was yesterday. Who am I today?'

'Why, one of us!' replies Gumbo. 'A long-in-the-
tooth cynic. It is true that I was not sold a bill of goods
like you, but I've managed to lose my self-respect just
the same. When I began writing for the *Word* I was as
bold as brass. I said what was what in no uncertain
manner. And had my copy cut to ribbons by the
censor's blue pencil. As I grew older and wiser I
learned to outwit the censor; at any rate my copy was
returned unamended. Of course I was fooling myself.
All I had learned was an ability to anticipate the blue
pencil, to censor myself in advance. If anything my
shame is greater than yours. At least you wrote from

the heart. I knew all along that I was peddling bullshit. So cheer up, Pumpkin, we're all in the same boat now.'

Being a literal-minded chap, I picture us all actually in a boat and am suddenly visited with a brainwave.

'If cars are too dangerous and aeroplanes out of the question,' I say, 'perhaps we can return to the motherland by sea.'

Gumbo leans across the table and plants a kiss on my forehead. 'It's brilliant in conception, rather like the late Marshal's political philosophy,' he says, 'but I'm afraid that Pumpkin's plan is going to be just as hard to put into practice. We cannot charter a vessel, because no one in their right mind would take us. Nor, I venture to guess, has any of us sailed any sort of boat outside of his bathtub.'

'Not true,' protests Chickpea. 'I once rented a pedalo for an hour and survived to tell the tale.'

'I have someone rather more experienced in mind,' I reply enigmatically.

•

Next morning Paprika comes to Endive in the form of a sirocco, which scours all exposed surfaces with water and red dust. I am awoken prematurely by the insistent whistling of the wind and, descending to get my money's-worth, find Odysseus and Telemachus already breakfasting upon salami and eggs.

'Do you mind if I join you?' I ask.

'It's a free country,' replies the former.

'Not if you're from Capsicum,' I respond.

Once seated I semaphore my need for coffee and, leaning forward, whisper conspiratorially: 'I still don't know the purpose of your journey, but if you are ready to quit this place, may I suggest that we leave together.'

'You're asking for another lift in the Zatopec?' says Telemachus.

'There's no safe way out of here by road,' I reply, 'but there might be by sea.'

Father and son exchange glances.

'You have a boat?' asks Telemachus, with unconcealed eagerness.

'Not exactly,' I reply, 'but I know of a suitable craft made temporarily redundant, and if your father is the man he says he is, he might be just the person to captain it.'

'Is there a crew?' asks Odysseus.

'No,' I say, 'but I can guarantee the services of four eager and able-bodied men.'

I sip my coffee, while Odysseus mops up the remainder of his yolk with a triangle of toast.

'Telemachus,' I say, 'I'm sorry I seemed so insensitive when you told me that your mother had died. I have since heard that my own is very sick. She has no one but me. That is why I am so anxious to return to Capsicum.'

Odysseus cuts a piece of fatty salami into quarters and nods.

'We're interested,' says Telemachus.

'The relevant party is keen,' I inform my fellow musketeers (soon to be buccaneers).

In other circumstances (viz. those pertaining the day before yesterday) the chances of hijacking the Marshal's yacht would have been less than zero. Now all it requires is the participation of a plump young prostitute from the red-light district, who easily monopolizes the attention of the yacht's indifferent and lonely guardian. While he pleasures himself at our expense, we sneak on board. It feels like sacrilege, but our progress continues unopposed; no voice or hand is raised against us. Only the yacht itself rocks, as if in protest against our trespass. And trespass it is as Gumbo, Chickpea, and Haricot discover smuggled caviar and champagne in the galley, Great Bear vodka in the icebox, pornographic videos on the bookshelves, sharp suits and silk shirts in the wardrobe, and top-secret dossiers everywhere else. Odysseus, needless to say, is more interested in the mechanics of our acquisition, acquainting himself with the global positioning system (imported from Buffalo) and the very high frequency Sailor radio. I sneak away, unnoticed, and (locked behind a concertina door) commit the greatest sacrilege of all in the Marshal's head. The water in the toilet bowl (which now resembles a slice of toast spread with clear honey) suddenly vibrates, and the whole vessel begins to throb with life. I immediately button my flies and proceed directly to the helm. A damp wind is still blowing from the east, stirring the waters and making wavelets even within the harbour wall. Anchored boats creak as they ride the swell, their slack ropes cracking like whips. Otherwise the marina is strangely quiet, seemingly devoid of all human activity. Unhindered Telemachus casts off the moorings, and the Marshal's erstwhile yacht, now under new command, is slowly absorbed by the turbulent night.

If the local constabulary were unconcerned by the enormity of our transgression, the elements seem determined to make good their omission, to ensure that we do not escape unpunished. Huge breakers greet us as soon as we hit the open sea.

'Up to your old tricks, eh, Poseidon?' roars Odysseus, as he steers his craft up the next wave's perpendicular flanks. But even while we are still climbing it, the wave sweeps on and we descend rapidly to sea level, which remains level only until the next wave appears.

'Hope you've all got good sea-legs,' laughs Odysseus, his beard already dripping.

It is a forlorn hope. Within minutes Haricot is green. Chickpea chuckles unsympathetically, only to become jaundiced himself moments afterwards. Both make for the railings, where they are soon joined by a bilious Gumbo.

'It's a great set of men you've found me, Mr Pumpkin,' yells Odysseus. 'I trust I can still count on you at least.'

Being a sailor of the old school he prefers to use the stars for guidance, but since the sky is completely overcast he sends me below to raid the chart locker.

My attempt to descend the steps coincides with our ascent of a movable Kilimanjaro, so that I actually find it necessary to step up in order to go down. The destabilization continues on the lower deck, where the floor suddenly becomes a wall. As I proceed I feel the blood drain from my face. My saliva vanishes as completely as if I had just gargled with deodorant. Although I am shivering, I begin to sweat. Stumbling into a cabin, I remain immobilized for several eternities until I feel sufficiently well to vomit. I continue to vomit with some frequency until the storm subsides some twenty hours later. Only then am I able to complete my task. More dead than alive I deliver the charts to Odysseus.

Fortunately he seems to have found his way to land without their assistance: before me I see a fertile island that rises from the sea like a gigantic foot. The sun is low behind it, covering the distant hills with a crimson wash and staining the sea mauve. Large jellyfish, each stamped with a facsimile of the human physiognomy, drift upon its placid surface trailing glassy petticoats. Closer scrutiny confirms that appearances can often deceive: the jellyfish are not jellyfish but a strict order of nuns, permitted an evening dip so long as they shed neither habit nor wimple. We skirt the beach and join a fleet of returning fishing smacks. Its crewmen are too busy gutting their catch and disposing of all the unwanted innards to show any interest in a gate-crasher (however incongruous). They seem equally impervious to the stink that pollutes their wake and threatens to send me back to the privy. The screeching gulls have no such scruples.

'This is Sardinia, isn't it?' I say to Odysseus.

'What makes you think that?' he replies.

'Because I did geography at school,' I reply, 'so I know where the sun sets. I also know the name of the biggest island west of Ancho. What I don't know is why we aren't sailing north. Either we're badly off course, or you have no intention of taking us back to Capsicum. Which is it?'

'I'll assume that this is not mutiny but an honest enquiry,' replies Odysseus. 'So I'll give a straight answer. Within minutes of starting our journey I observed that our fuel tanks were dangerously low. Your friends were feeding the fishes. You had gone on an errand and not returned. I had to make a choice. Should I refuel in a port populated by bloodthirsty Anchovies, or should I make a detour to the neutral kingdom of Sardinia? Would you have done otherwise, Mr Pumpkin?'

It is an unimpeachable argument, yet I know that Odysseus is a sly man and cannot be rid of the suspicion that he is harbouring a secret.

As we speak Odysseus manoeuvres the yacht into an empty berth, whereupon young Telemachus leaps ashore and performs origami with the ropes. Odysseus nods in the direction of his ineffectual crew, huddled on the deck like the survivors of a shipwreck, and says: 'May I suggest that you and your friends recover your equilibrium on shore, and then (if you develop sufficient energy) join the other lusty sailors in painting the town red. Meanwhile we will refuel and purchase sufficient supplies for our voyage. Enjoy yourself, Mr Pumpkin, but whatever you do make sure you are on board before sunrise. We sail at dawn.'

The four buccaneers, thus encouraged, stagger down the gangplank and are quickly revived by salty air and the relative stability of solid ground beneath their feet. Innumerable barrels of silver fish line the waterfront, as well as tubs stuffed with crabs still active enough to open and close their claws. Some even manage to o'erleap the rim and, regaining the cobbles, make futile attempts to evade the saucepan of boiling water that awaits. The shoppers seem to regard these small invertebrate tragedies as risible; at any rate, all transactions are completed with determined grins upon the faces of both buyers and sellers. 'What we need is rum,' says Gumbo, 'a glass of dark rum for every man, to revive the appetite.' Since practically every building we pass is fronted by a smiling barker extolling the virtues of his establishment's pickled fish and fire water we are soon as merry as the locals.

'Wow,' says Chickpea, as he downs his fifth in the musky interior of the Codpiece, 'the monsoon season has arrived big-time. Haricot, lead me to the pissoir.'

Gumbo also rises. 'Are you going to join us?' he enquires of me.

'I'm fine,' I say. 'Don't forget I spent the entire night in the lavatory.'

When they return I can tell that a plan has been hatched.

'Are you married, Pumpkin?' asks Gumbo.

'Not yet,' I reply cautiously.

'Well I am, as are Chickpea and Haricot (and not to each other),' he says. 'Our marital status notwithstanding, we all three feel the urgent need for some traditional rest and recreation. Have you ever enjoyed the services of a prostitute, Pumpkin?'

'Never,' I reply.

'In that case, tonight will be my treat,' cries Gumbo. 'It will be my privilege to initiate you into the demimonde.'

'Not before we've had a last round for the road,' I say.

'Oh man,' says the bartender, 'your dog just died or something? If you don't pin a smile to your face the Sockeye will snatch you for sure.'

'The Sockeye?' I say.

'Man, you really are a stranger,' he says. 'Everyone knows about the Sockeye. The long arm of King Salmon the Twenty-third. Sardinia's secret police. The aforementioned king is a mite peculiar; paranoid you might even think. Not to smile is regarded by him as a sign of discontent. Discontent is regarded as one step short of rebellion. Those caught scowling are dragged away and tortured. Tortured until they laugh at the pain. To avoid this misfortune we all wear fixed grins. I'd advise you to do as we all do and chew on this.' He slides a plastic bag across the counter. 'Crowfoot. Chew it long enough and it causes a rictus that stretches the upper lip and exposes the teeth; in short, the world-famous sardonic smile. Born not of happiness or pleasure, but of fear.'

I slip the packet into my pocket, intending to reserve the leaves for the brothel so that I will be sure of exiting with a smile of satisfaction on my face. 'Oh, and four rums,' I say.

'What a strange place this is,' I inform my companions. 'They arrest you for looking miserable.'

'Then we had better get laid immediately,' cries Gumbo, downing his rum in a single gulp.

The port, we discover, has a brothel for every week of the year. The one Gumbo selects – for he is undoubtedly our leader on this occasion, our master of hounds – has a red door and creaking stairs. Even I feel a frisson of excitement as we mount them, heading for the light at the top and the unknown delights it will illuminate. Inside a grinning giant from darkest Paprika is playing a hyperactive boogie-woogie on an upright piano, while a dozen pretty harlots in transparent negligees or undies recline languorously on velvet sofas. Some are lost in private reveries. Others play patience. One is reading a book.

'Pumpkin has first pick,' announces Gumbo. 'Who is it to be?'

I immediately select the reader, select her because she wears glasses and has a broken nose, and consequently seems the least threatening of them all. Select her because she looks like she would probably prefer to discuss literature rather than make unreasonable demands upon my manhood.

'Funny book?' I ask, forgetting that smiles are mandatory.

'Hardly,' she replies, tossing the lurid paperback aside, and removing her glasses. So much for my ability to judge people at a glance.

Her room is bare save for a double bed with a scarlet

spread, a dresser, and a small table, upon which stands a brass lamp and a half-empty bottle of grappa. In an unlit alcove I notice a toilet and a small sink. The whore sits on the side of the bed and begins to remove her stockings. The only other garments preserving her modesty are a pair of knickers and a chemise. I definitely want her to dispose of them, but I am also dreading the moment when she does, for her nakedness will be my cue to perform. And I confess to stage fright. Her fingers isolate the hem of her vest, and she slowly raises it over her head. Her exposed breasts rise and fall with the movement. Then she stands and unceremoniously pulls down her pants, which she kicks across the room. So the rumours are true, women really do have pubic hair down there. I am more surprised to discover that they only have one nipple. I'd heard whispers about pubic hair, but never a word about that. My stare lasts a moment too long.

'Do I displease you?' asks the whore.

I shake my head. 'I was just wondering about the nipple,' I mumble, 'wondering why it's in the singular.'

Suddenly her smile seems uncomfortably at odds with the misery manifest in her eyes. 'All prostitutes must have a nipple removed, by order of King Salmon the Twenty-third,' she explains, 'lest any man marry one of us in ignorance. They call it a mark of shame, we prefer to call it the badge of our guild.'

Still I hesitate, the Hamlet of the boudoir.

'Would you rather watch me masturbate?' asks the whore.

'No,' I say, 'I'd really like to fuck you.' If not now, when?

For the first time in my adult life I remove all my clothes in front of a woman.

'Come here,' she says when I am in my prelapsarian state. She is certainly no beauty, but her breasts are large and her loins are uncovered, so I hold her tightly and experience the unique comfort of flesh on flesh.

'Come,' she says, leading me to the bed, 'let us lie side by side.'

Thanks to the laws of censorship imposed by the puritanical Marshal, I have never seen a couple demonstrate the art of love on the big screen, and consequently have no idea what to do next. Because her breasts are both inviting and easily available I decide to experiment with them first. She groans encouragingly, so I assume I've done the right thing. She is even more enthusiastic – frighteningly so – when I insert a finger between her thighs.

'Shall I touch you?' she asks.

'Please,' I say.

'Don't you like me?' she asks, obviously disappointed by the lifeless thing she has found beached beneath the white cliff of my belly.

'I like you a lot,' I reply, 'but I'm very nervous.'

'Of me?' she exclaims incredulously. 'I'm not even a woman. I'm a tart.' She pauses. 'I'm your first, aren't I?'

'Woman or tart?'

'You tell me.'

'Both.'

'Am I to understand that you're still a virgin?'

I look away, but I nod.

'How is that possible? You're hardly in the first flush of youth.'

'I'm overweight and I've always been unattractive to women,' I say. 'At university my fellow students all lost their virginity, but I couldn't give mine away. Then the moment passed, and in time I became too embarrassed to redeem it.'

'That's the saddest story I ever heard,' says the whore, still trying valiantly to raise the dead. She rubs. She sucks. She even rams a finger up my rectum, which makes me gasp.

'Do you really want me to go on?' she asks.

'More than anything else in the world,' I reply.

'Don't go away,' she says, 'I'll be back in a minute.'

Without even bothering to cover her nakedness she leaves the room. I remain, utterly humiliated, too ashamed even to invent legends of my prowess that will impress my fellow buccaneers, who are – even now – making the bed-springs groan all over the house. My patient whore returns with a clay bowl full of plum-sized goodies. 'Eat of the fruit,' says the whore.

I gather one gingerly. Its skin is rust-coloured and leathery, but the flesh beneath is soft and has the shade and modest sheen of unpolished amber. I bite, releasing a tear that is both sweet and sharp. The juice is refreshing and has an addictive property that compels me to empty the bowl. The whore, meanwhile, has begun to whisper obscenities in my ear.

'Are you a big boy?' she hisses. 'Because mama needs a big boy to fill her jelly roll.'

'Then mama's in luck,' someone roars, 'because I'm a fucking giant.'

The intervention surprises me, because I did not think there was anyone else in the room.

'Who was that?' I ask.

'The only real man on the premises,' replies the whore.

Somehow the brute lifts me bodily and dumps me on top of the trollop. 'Now let's play hunt the salami,' he guffaws. He hides it in her belly. Then he flips her around and hides it up her back passage. He even hides it right in the middle of her stupid smile.

'One thing's for sure,' gasps the whore, wiping her mouth, 'a virgin you ain't. Not any more.'

'But it was the other man who fucked you,' I protest.

'What other man? There is no one in here but the two of us.'

I am confused. What if I am not the me I always thought I was, but another me altogether? Either way, I need a slash. The bedspread, I note as I rise, is scattered with shards of skin and gleaming brown stones that resemble goat turds.

'What the devil are those?' I ask.

'Don't you remember?' asks the whore. 'They are the remains of the jujubes you ate.'

'Jujubes? What the hell are jujubes?'

'A speciality of the region,' she replies.

I aim at the water and direct a torrent into the pan. Having shaken the drips from my cock, I turn around and nearly jump out of my skin. A gaunt old biddy is watching me.

'Are you trying to give me a fucking heart attack?' I yell, on the assumption that she's an ex-whore given a sinecure as the working whore's maid.

'When I begged you not to come home,' says the grim old baggage, 'I didn't mean that you should turn your back on it altogether.'

Home? What is the hag talking about? This room is my home. All I require is here: a big bed and a naked whore. My heart's desire.

'You certainly seem determined to make up for lost time,' observes the whore, as I enter her conventionally for the fourth time. Even before I have finished three new customers enter.

'Hey,' I shout, 'get outside and wait your turn.'

'Who would have thought that our gentle com-

panion would have proved to be such a beast in bed,'
says Two to Three.

'Not me,' agrees Three.

'Pumpkin,' says One, 'it's time to go. Odysseus
doesn't really need us. And he won't wait.'

Pumpkin? Odysseus? The names mean nought to
me. 'I don't know who you are, and I don't know what
you're talking about,' I yell, 'so just fuck off and let
me get on with it.'

Next thing I know they're pulling me away from
the whore. Two hold me down, while the third dresses
me as best he can. Then they drag me down the stairs
and into the street. A few early risers are about, but
none is prepared to lift a finger in my defence. Instead
they draw bananas in the air. Several mouth a single
word: 'Sockeye.' They assume, I suppose, that I am
under arrest. In which case why have I been frog-
marched to the harbour rather than a prison? The
answer becomes manifest when I am bundled on to a
grand yacht flying an unknown flag: I have obviously
fallen into the hands of a merciless press gang. As I
am thrown into a dark cabin and hear my captors lock
the door, I know in my heart that I shall never see my
beloved whore again.

•

On the third night of my unjust incarceration I unexpectedly begin to miss the mother I never knew I had.

And once I have a mother I must (by definition) have a self, and this self obviously has a name; thus Pumpkin is reborn, already in his majority. Before I hammer on the door to advertise the good news, I peer through the porthole in hopes of ascertaining our whereabouts, but there is no hint in the black sea, nor do I possess the expertise to decipher the stars above. There is something else in the darkness, however, something barely visible. I watch as an unlit fishing boat becomes apparent, watch nonplussed as it silently draws alongside our stern, whereupon a fellow in a balaclava casts a muffled grappling hook over our rail and (armed with a Kalashnikov) swings himself on board. Moments later a dozen of his fierce comrades follow his lead and land lightly on our upper deck. I begin to panic. I may be a landlubber, but I know pirates when I see them. Having identified the intruders I am at a loss as to what I should do next. Should I alert my companions to their immediate danger, thereby exposing myself to the same? Or should I keep mum, in hopes of escaping with my life? A short burst of machine-gun fire helps me come to a quick decision.

There's no more shooting, but a lot of shouting, and half a dozen alarming thwacks and thuds. More shouting, then the boat unmistakably changes course. Shortly thereafter I hear the shuffling of many feet, followed by a firmer step in the corridor outside. Doors open and close until (at last) the dread moment arrives, and my handle begins to turn. But being locked my door refuses to open.

'What's in the mizzen cabin?' barks the frustrated pirate.

'Nothing,' replies Odysseus.

'A better answer,' says the pirate, 'or someone dies.'

'Very well,' says Odysseus. 'A crewman lost his mind. We have him locked in there for his own good.'

'Show me,' says the pirate.

And so Odysseus unlocks the door, and a bold free-booter kicks it open. Within its frame I see my fellow travellers, blindfolded and bound, surrounded by their masked captors. Foaming at the mouth I throw myself to the ground, and clasp the legs of the leading brigand. 'My saviour,' I cry, 'have you found it?'

'Found what?' he demands eagerly.

'That which I have lost,' I reply. He pushes me aside.

'Lock him up with the rest,' he orders. It's an improvement; at least I'll have company now.

Unfortunately the uneasy atmosphere in our make-shift prison does nothing to raise our spirits. Odysseus is furious and he expects all of us to cower like fearful curs.

'Where were the lookouts?' he growls. 'Did you think I was joking when I warned that notorious pirates prowl these waters?' If his arms were not bound

he would surely have strangled Haricot and Chickpea
(the narcoleptic offenders) with his bare hands.

'Let's have a little less of the self-righteousness,' I
say, breaking the fearful silence; 'we would never have
encountered the pirates if we had not strayed into their
domain, which (if I am not mistaken) is the open sea
to the west of Sardinia. Why are you so determined to
chase the setting sun, Odysseus? Had you but kept
to our agreed course we would be halfway home by
now, rather than at the mercy of cut-throats.'

'Well said, Pumpkin,' cries Gumbo.

'Perhaps it would be better if we stopped blaming
each other and worked together,' adds Telemachus.

'The boy's spot on,' agrees Gumbo. 'Don't forget
our motto: one for all, and all for one!'

It occurs to me, somewhat ungraciously, that I
might be better off if they had forgotten it and left me
in the bordello. Nevertheless, I thank them for their
trouble.

'What got into you, Pumpkin?' asks Gumbo.

'No idea,' I reply. 'One minute I'm my familiar self,
the next I'm a creature of sensation, lacking both
memory and expectation. When you three showed up
it was as if three complete strangers had entered the
room.'

'I'll tell you what happened,' says Odysseus. 'You
fell in with a lotus-eater and became one yourself.
I am to blame, I should have warned you. I must

also, as Mr Pumpkin points out, accept responsibility for our present predicament.'

'What do you think will happen to us?' asks Gumbo.

'Nothing too dreadful,' replies Odysseus. 'If they had intended to kill us they would certainly have done so already. The fact that they haven't means that we are of more value to them as booty.'

'Booty?'

'Yes,' replies Odysseus, 'they undoubtedly intend to sell us as slaves.'

Obviously I am no less worried about my long-term future than the others, but I have a more pressing and urgent concern: the fact that I am pregnant with piss. Our blindfolds are never removed, not even for necessary forays to the lavatory. These are not made according to individual needs, but collectively at specific times of the day (morning and evening, one assumes, but it is impossible to be precise, given the constant darkness of our existence). Anyway, we are marched in single file (a pirate fore and aft) and made to stand in a line outside the water closet. As you know my sphincter turns bolshie when subject to pressure, and all I have managed thus far is a feeble squirt or two. But then it is a very regressive situation. Blindfolded and permanently bound I stand as helpless as a babe, while a pirate (reeking of tobacco, alcohol, and fish oil) unbuttons my flies, and with a calloused hand pulls out my wrinkled dick. My humiliation is

compounded when our minder returns to flush the
bowl and finds the water still pristine. Nevertheless, I
rise hopefully whenever a pirate enters in the vain
expectation that this time I will be able to drain the
reservoir that weighs as heavily on my lower abdomen
as a watermelon. On this occasion, however, we tread
an unfamiliar path, and (having climbed a ladder) feel
the sun upon our sightless faces.

There is little doubt that we are nearing the end of
our involuntary voyage. The engines have ceased to
throb, and the yacht is barely moving. Moreover, I can
hear the various sounds of rejoicing mingling with the
silvery regurgitations of pelagic birds, an impression
confirmed when my blindfold is rudely snatched from
my forehead and a sandy bay with a single jetty slowly
comes into focus. The mother ship, on closer inspection a weather-beaten tramp steamer with a pea-green
funnel, is already unloading. However loathsome our
kidnappers are to us, they are clearly heroes in their
home port; champions of the downtrodden and the
meek of the earth, if their welcome is anything to go
by. As they disembark, little girls in embroidered
blouses and skirts place garlands around the necks of
the captain and his entire pack of feral sea dogs. The
local men, meanwhile, congregate around the Marshal's erstwhile cruiser, shaking their heads in wonder
and delight at its magnificence and the audacity of
its conquerors. When our turn comes to set foot upon

terra incognita we are completely ignored, with the notable exception of Telemachus. As we proceed, he alone receives the admiring glances of females (both young and old), all of whom fervently wish they had the wherewithal to purchase him.

'Perhaps they would treat us with more respect,' I remark to Odysseus (the calmest amongst us), 'if they knew that we – having stolen the accursed boat in the first place – were also members of the criminal fraternity.'

Thus far we have only seen the chief author of our woes from a distance, but as we leave the hyperactive waterfront and enter the shanty town proper, he suddenly appears in our path as if from nowhere.

'My name is Captain Mandragora,' he says, bowing low, 'and I bid you welcome.' He is a brute of a man with a leonine mane of fiery hair and matching beard, like Odysseus gone wild, or Barbarossa reincarnate.

'And I am Odysseus,' says my companion, 'whose journey you have inconsiderately interrupted. If your manners are any more than display you will speed me on my way immediately. Perhaps with gifts as a sign of respect.'

Captain Mandragora roars with laughter. 'Respect you will have to earn,' he says, 'but I like you already. There is always a feast to mark our safe return. Tonight will be no exception. You and your tongue-tied companions will sit at my table.'

Journey? What journey? Were we sailing to Capsicum, or were we sailing elsewhere? If so, why and
where?

'Permit me to escort you to your new quarters,' says
Captain Mandragora, dismissing our guards with a nod
of his great head.

The town, through which we are marching, is
obviously old, if not exactly ancient. Nearly all its
buildings are domestic, simple dwellings covered with
plaster (now cracking or worse) and washed with rose
madder. A few are graced with fragile balconies,
wrought-iron tangles that have grown a second scaly
skin. Nevertheless, they remain secure enough to
support the property's inhabitants, who salute the
returning hero with unforced zeal. Pedestrians, too,
greet Captain Mandragora with such unrestrained joy
that even he seems slightly perplexed. The Marshal in
his heyday surely never received a warmer welcome
in the streets of Capsicum. Soon the densely populated
part of the port is behind us, and we find ourselves
passing through a sweet-scented valley dotted with red
roofed villas. Overlooking them all, atop the largest of
the hills, stands a more palatial structure.

'The house of Mandragora,' says our leader,
unnecessarily.

Perhaps the locals are anticipating the official feast,
or perhaps there is another cause for celebration; either
way, the valley is filled with groups of young men

roasting sheep over open fires. So many gilded youths for such a small community! Their arrogance is such that (unlike their urban cousins) they fail even to acknowledge our party, let alone invite us to enjoy a slice of the roasting flesh (the aroma of which is certainly making my mouth water).

'Who are all these ill-mannered whippersnappers,' grumbles Captain Mandragora, 'and who gave them permission to slaughter my flock in such numbers?'

As we approach ever nearer the house on the hill, the subtle song of the Sardinian warblers and the hoo-hoo-hoo of the hoopoes are overwhelmed by the sound of electric guitars and caterwauling escaping from its open doors and windows. Captain Mandragora's pace increases, and the look on his face gradually changes from confusion to anger. This is further provoked by the discovery that the watchtowers, which rise above the wooden palisade at regular intervals, are all entirely unmanned. Nor is the impregnable gate even bolted. Only a hound, the size of a small bear, acknowledges his master's arrival. So unexpected is it that when a young woman finally appears she takes one look at him and faints dead away.

'Haidee!' cries Captain Mandragora. 'Whatever is it? Whatever is the matter?'

So saying he leaps to her assistance with astonishing agility, but young Telemachus is even swifter and manages to catch the girl's head before it can bounce even once upon the marble floor. He cradles his prize in the crook of his arm; as a consequence his face is the first thing she sees when she reopens her lovely eyes. She examines her saviour's fine features, then reluctantly (or so it seems to me) turns her attention to the master of the house.

'Papa,' she says, still propped up by Telemachus, 'forgive this foolishness and my lack of faith, but it was whispered that you were dead; that unknown gunships had sunk your boat and blasted its bold captain and crew to kingdom come. Nor did any word arrive to contradict the rumours.'

'Foolish girl,' chides her father, 'how could you have forgotten the golden rule: no contact with home during raids, lest the authorities locate our hideout? You should also have remembered that the comings and goings of pirates are not dictated by timetables. So your father is not late, in either sense of the word. Now come and welcome him properly.'

Telemachus helps the distressed maiden to an upright position, and then (brushing him aside) she totters across the vestibule to embrace her resurrected sire. The boy cannot take his eyes off her. No wonder! Her long legs are barely concealed by silken pantaloons, while an embroidered brassiere strains to contain the pulchritude it conceals. Her nut-brown midriff sparkles with gold dust, and a band of pearls encircles her coppery curls. As we witness the tearful reunion, more young men (obviously attracted by the commotion) appear from the shadows and fill the hall.

'Do not fret, my pigeon,' says the fierce pirate, 'your papa is hale and hearty. And very, very rich. Or he was until these parasites appeared. Tell me, Haidee, who are all these strangers? And what is their purpose?'

'Who are they?' echoes the beautiful odalisque. 'Why, they are my suitors, of course. Hearing that you were at the bottom of the sea they insisted upon paying me court (at my expense), and have refused to leave until I have chosen my husband from amongst them.' The old story.

•

Our prison has no bars, nor any locks (except on the bathroom doors, I am relieved to note). In fact within the estate we are barely confined at all, making it easy for us to forget our true status.

'Comfortable rooms, nice view,' says Chickpea. 'It's a bit like being on vacation.'

'Nor do they intend to let us starve,' adds Haricot, contemplating tonight's feast.

'Of course not,' comments Odysseus. 'It is in their interest to fatten us up. No one will fork out for a skinny slave.'

Some of the suitors, getting wind of Captain Mandragora's unanticipated return, chicken out of the banquet, but the bolder take their usual places around the numerous tables in the great hall. His profession notwithstanding, Captain Mandragora displays dainty table manners, dissecting his sea bass with the delicacy of an anatomist. Nor does he drink to excess, imbibing no more than a single bottle of claret. Most of the suitors are not so abstemious; rum and wine soon loosen their tongues and their morals. They molest the modest serving girls as they distribute the meat course, the salsify and the rice, and they continually pollute their conversation with *double entendres*.

Only one of their number behaves with any decorum. But then he alone seems possessed of a strategy. He has inveigled himself into a seat beside Captain Mandragora, with whom he is deep in conversation. He listens intently, but his thoughts are clearly elsewhere, judging by the fact that his eyes constantly return to the voluptuous figure of his host's treasured daughter.

'I assume you know who that is,' murmurs Gumbo.

'Of course,' I say. 'I'd know that flushed physiognomy and bleached crop anywhere. It's Radish, the Marshal's only son.'

'He looks like a prick to me,' remarks Telemachus, viciously slicing his lamb.

'I'm sure you're right,' says Gumbo. 'He has an unenviable reputation as an especially cruel and dissolute playboy.'

'Even so I can't but feel a little sympathy for the boy,' says Chickpea. 'He's had one big shock already today, when his fiancée's father came back from the dead and put paid to his immediate expectations. He's due for an even worse one when we inform him that his own father – whom he obviously thinks of as still hearty and all-powerful – has been blown away like smoke.'

'Leaving him no legacy but division and strife,' adds Haricot.

'We'll have to pick our moment to break the news very carefully,' muses Gumbo.

Odysseus leans across the table. 'Why have you taken against that particular young man so strongly?' he demands of his son.

•

Maybe it's because the night is so sultry, or maybe it's because I have devoured too much red meat and swallowed too much rough wine; either way, I cannot sleep. So I rise from my tousled bed and wander aimlessly around the grounds of Castle Mandragora until I find myself at the summit of the hill on which it stands. Below me, blanketed by night, lies the outlaw state entire: its compact territory, its tiny capital, and its rocky coastline. There is no cooling breeze and the surrounding water moves to its own sluggish rhythm, like ink trembling in anticipation of the master's pen.

I note that my own hands are less than steady. Captain Mandragora may not have the power to create brave new worlds, but he can certainly alter ours for good or ill with a single word. Perhaps it is this uncomfortable knowledge which keeps me awake.

Proceeding, I note that I am not the island's sole insomniac. Walking towards me is a shapely woman draped in white. Not a ghost, nor a virgin bride with pre-connubial jitters, but the blessed daughter of the house. What keeps Haidee from her innocent slumber? Something is certainly worrying her. Her gait is that of the sleepwalker or zombie, and she remains utterly blind to my presence until our paths actually cross, whereupon she emits a delightful squeak. At first her face registers horror, then (recognizing me as one of the slaves-in-waiting) she smiles so sweetly that I would willingly proffer her my freedom on a plate.

'You gave me quite a start, Mr — ' she says.

'Pumpkin,' I say, filling in the blank.

'Poor Mr Pumpkin,' she croons, 'I dare say you have your own worries.'

'Meaning that you too have yours?' I speculate.

'You have guessed correctly, Mr Pumpkin,' she says, rubbing her unlined forehead. 'Like yours, mine will not let me sleep.'

'I am unable to help myself,' I say, 'but perhaps I can help you? If only by listening.'

'You would be well within your rights to do me –

the helpless daughter of your kidnapper – all manner of harm,' she notes. 'But you have not raised a finger against me. Obviously you are a gentle man, Mr Pumpkin, but are you one that I may trust?'

Placing my hand on my heart I utter the following oath: 'I swear on my mother's life that I will never betray you.'

'It's like this, Mr Pumpkin,' says Haidee. 'Last night my father entered the great hall fully intending to rout the suitors and send them all packing. He would have done so, too, if it had not been for the poisonous Radish. In return for my hand that creature has offered him and all his cronies a general amnesty, as well as a commission in his father's navy. As a consequence, newly appointed Admiral Mandragora intends to announce our engagement tomorrow night, in front of the assembled suitors. Perhaps it would not have seemed such a tragedy yesterday, before I met the man of my dreams. Oh, unlucky Haidee! To glimpse love and have it snatched away, all in the compass of a single day. Mr Pumpkin, will you help me? Will you save me from my inevitable fate? Or am I doomed to become Mrs Radish?' She translates my silence correctly. 'I thought as much,' she says. 'How could you? How could anyone? But you can certainly do one last thing for me. Before you finally retire, please inform Telemachus that I am not abed. And tell him where he may find me.'

Retracing my steps to the open prison that is our temporary home, I dig my hands deep in my pockets and feel a forgotten packet at the bottom of the left one. It takes a few moments for me to recall its provenance, and its properties.

•

Among the lesser loot acquired during the raid that also netted us is an antique dinner service made in the Orient of the finest bone china. Arising with the sun I wander into the kitchen and find the servants already hard at work sorting it in preparation for the night's hastily arranged celebration. It is universally supposed that an important announcement will be made, and most assume that it will concern the future of their gentle mistress. The suitors are discussed and examined as if they were runners in a steeplechase. Although one is the clear favourite to pass the post first, neither he nor any of the others is considered anywhere near good enough for the pirate's daughter.

'If only that handsome boy were a contender,' sighs one.

'What's his name?' asks another.

'Telemachus,' says a third dreamily, polishing the interior of a soup bowl. I note that it has its own lid, to prevent heat loss, from which I deduce that the consommé, or broth, or whatever, will be served in individual portions rather than from a collective tureen.

In the post-meridiem I seek out Haidee.

'Are you absolutely certain you don't want to marry Radish?' I ask.

'I hate him,' she replies firmly. 'Besides,' she adds with a knowing smile, 'after what happened last night it would be bigamy.'

'If my intervention is a success we will have an opportunity to escape from this place,' I say. 'Are you really prepared to flee with us, to leave all that you have known behind?'

'Despite my father's wicked ways I love him dearly,' replies Haidee, 'and I shall miss him till my last breath, but Telemachus is my husband now, and wither he goes I must follow.' Haidee then leans forward, cups my head between her warm hands, and kisses me firmly on my blushing cheek. 'Oh, Mr Pumpkin,' she cries, 'I always knew that I could count on you.'

Just before we enter the great hall I inform the others of my plan, and tell Gumbo of his essential role.

'How can you be so confident that it will work?' asks wily Odysseus, obviously miffed that so unprepossessing a figure has usurped his role as artful dodger.

'Because I am an excellent judge of human nature,' I reply (with slightly more assurance than I feel).

Since there is no love lost between the serving girls

and the suitors, it takes little persuading to gain privileged access to the bowl destined for Radish. Lifting its lid I carefully add an extra ingredient. 'I hope you are poisoning the shit,' hisses the waitress. 'I'll be the first to spit on his corpse. And believe me, I won't be the last.'

Only then does it occur to me that Radish might not like bouillabaisse, or might be allergic to seafood, or garlic, or might just not fancy fish soup at the moment. The list of imponderables over which I have no control is beginning to seem endless. Self-doubt begins to seep through me, like the crowfoot in the bouillon. Who am I kidding? I am an extra, not a man of destiny. How can I, the least significant Pumpkin who ever lived, even think of trying to outfox not only the most ferocious pirate in the Mediterranean, but also the late Marshal's demonic seed? I picture Haidee's face as it was when we parted, a portrait made of love and expectation. I picture it as it will be after the failure of my false promise, and wonder where I can best hide from the vengeful hand of the broken-hearted.

Taking my place between Chickpea and Haricot I watch helplessly as the waitress offers the soup bowl to Radish, and breathe a little easier when he carelessly nods assent. And so the bowl (that repository of all our hopes) is lowered, but before it actually reaches the table Radish twists sharply in his seat and inserts his right hand beneath the girl's skirt, as if daring her to tip the bowl's contents into his lap (which is already covered with a napkin), but she (bless her) barely flinches (even though his fingers are clearly violating her privacy) and completes the delivery. Having wiped his hand on his napkin, Radish raises the lid, sniffs the contents, whispers something vulgar to his neighbour, lifts his spoon, dips it, and (hallelujah) swallows the first mouthful. The first of many.

Captain Mandragora rises to his feet in the hiatus between the soup and the pasta course.

'Friends, fellow pirates, honoured guests,' he begins, 'I have two items of good news to share with you all. Both concern Mr Radish, the most persistent and the most audacious of all my daughter's suitors. I must begin this little oration by confessing that my initial response to the presence of Mr Radish and his peers was far from favourable; to tell you the truth, I thought them ill-bred, noisy scroungers. But Mr Radish has a very persuasive tongue. Especially when he speaks in his father's name; a patriarch who is but one step from the gods. In the end he changed my mind with a single word. The word was "amnesty". Yes, my dear friends and fellow fighters, acting with the full authority of his father, the Marshal, Mr Radish has offered us a general amnesty. All crimes are to be pardoned, not excepting rape and murder.'

The audience gasps, then applauds enthusiastically. Radish, smiling, takes a bow. More applause, until Captain Mandragora raises his hands, requesting silence.

'There is more, my friends,' he continues. 'I am to be made an admiral in the Marshal's navy, while you others will be guaranteed at least a captaincy.' There is greater applause, augmented by the banging of knives on the table-tops.

'That concludes the first part of my announcement,' he says. There follows an uncomfortable pause, as if the speaker is reluctant to continue. 'The second concerns the future of my beloved daughter,' he adds at last. 'In short, I have agreed to look favourably upon Mr Radish's wish to marry her. As of this minute they are officially betrothed. Please stand and raise your glasses, so that we may toast the future of the happy couple . . .' Radish grins from ear to ear, while poor Haidee looks as if the sky has just fallen upon her.

I tap Gumbo on the shoulder. Resisting the general merriment he throws his champagne flute to the ground (where it shatters) and cries: 'Has the Marshal actually signed any of the said amnesties?'

'Not yet,' replies Radish happily.

'Then he never will,' snaps Gumbo, 'because the old man is as dead as mutton.'

Radish greets the bombshell with his buoyant smile

intact. 'Nonsense,' he yells, 'how could so mighty an oak fall, and the whole forest not know of it?'

'In such a place as this ignorance is the norm,' responds Gumbo. 'May I remind you that your bride-to-be thought her own father dead until he stood before her yesterday.'

'That is certainly true,' comments Captain Mandragora.

Radish, clearly flustered, is making heroic efforts to annul his inappropriate facial expression, but try as he might his upper lip remains tightly stretched, permanently exposing his nicotine-stained teeth beneath.

'What is the meaning of that idiotic smile?' demands Captain Mandragora. 'Surely the announcement of a father's death – even if false – is not a suitable cause for mirth.'

Radish, utterly confused, can do nothing but cover his mouth with his right hand.

'Time for the *coup de grâce*,' I whisper to Gumbo.

'Perhaps we should consider the possibility that Mr Radish's involuntary smile has another – more sinister – cause,' he says. 'Remember that he never actually denied that his father was dead, he simply said that he would certainly be aware of the fact if he was. And the fact is that he is. Would amateurs like us really have been able to hijack the Marshal's yacht if he were otherwise? In which case Mr Radish's promises, so rashly made, stink of bad faith, because he knows very well his father can never honour them. At best he intends to make fools of you, to laugh at you behind your backs. But there is a worse possibility, a much worse possibility.' Gumbo pauses, turns to face his host, then continues thus: 'Captain Mandragora, I fear that your daughter's victorious suitor intends to have you and your men arrested as soon as you set foot on the mainland. Furthermore, I believe that he plans to secure his uncertain succession with a show trial, to be followed by your summary execution.' The fact that Radish is now brazenly displaying a full-blown sardonic smile does nothing to help his cause.

Captain Mandragora pushes his chair aside, walks directly to his would-be son-in-law, and grabs him by the lapels of his satin jacket.

'I know of one way to wipe that accursed smile off your face,' he screams, lifting the lad with one hand and slapping him hard around the head with the other.

Released, the bruised youth staggers and groans, but his smile remains defiantly intact. A bright-red worm begins to wriggle out of his brain via his afflicted ear. Radish touches it disbelievingly, examines his finger, and still smiling cries: 'That bastard has made me bleed!' At which several of his sycophants draw pistols from concealed shoulder holsters.

Already the great hall has become pandemonium. Pirates and suitors alike jump from their places and overturn the heavy dinner tables, sending the bravely acquired crockery flying in all directions along with the freshly served spaghetti. The waitresses themselves flee to the kitchen or a nearer exit, their stiletto heels clicking on the flagstones. Now protected by thick oak, the pirates and the suitors begin firing deadly fusillades at each other. Straining to be heard over the cacophony of screams, smashing plates, falling cutlery, breaking glass, and fizzing bullets I cry: 'It's time we took our leave.'

'Not before I've rescued Haidee,' replies Telemachus, crawling across the floor in her direction.

When we were under fire at Pomodoro, Odysseus seemed impossibly calm. Nor did the fierce demeanour of Captain Mandragora ever upset his equanimity. But now he is unquestionably agitated. Why? Surely not because of selfish fears for his own skin? No, his uncharacteristic attack of nerves can only be explained by the fact that his beloved son is courting danger.

'Has Telemachus taken leave of his senses?' cries the legendary traveller become anguished father. 'Or is he so keen to meet his mother again that he seeks a short cut?'

'It is life, not death, that draws him,' I say. 'Telemachus has found his own Penelope.'

At any rate he has safely reached the table which shelters Haidee. Her father stands full-length beside her crouching figure, a smoking pistol in either hand.

He looks magnificent, as if posing for a memorial commissioned to honour some hero's last stand. Pushing his daughter from his side as she attempts to hug him, he gleefully peppers the trapped suitors with unsporting dum-dums. And so Haidee turns away from her father and, guided by her lover, begins the hazardous journey towards a new life.

Once we are outside the house her presence becomes decidedly beneficial, in particular when we reach the forbidding gate which separates Captain Mandragora's estate from the remainder of the island. Its guardians are far from keen to open it, until our delightful burden calms their suspicions with gentle authority. After that it's plain sailing 'neath a brilliant moon straight down to the harbour. News of the gun-fight at Castle Mandragora has obviously preceded us to the port, to the effect that all the able-bodied men have armed themselves and are hurrying to defend their endangered hydrarchy and its unquestioned leader. The ruffians posted to protect the Marshal's yacht are no exceptions; they too decide that they are better employed elsewhere. We take full advantage of their absence.

As the lights of the island slowly dissolve into the cappuccino night, I revel in my unaccustomed role as Pumpkin the Hero. Gumbo, Chickpea, and Haricot all come to pay their respects before retiring. Only Odysseus keeps his distance, sulking in the wheelhouse.

At first I am vain enough to think him jealous of me, resentful that I have usurped his place as trickster-in-chief. But then I observe Telemachus and Haidee embracing on the deck, and guess he is coming to terms with the realization that he is no longer the centre of his son's universe, that his boy is slipping away from his old orbit and beginning to revolve around a more heavenly body. Whereupon I begin to weep softly, not in pity for the abandoned father, but out of remorse for my own crime. Pumpkin, I demand of myself, when did you last think of your mother? This is followed by the unbearable conviction that she has taken her final breath in the meantime, died without so much as the comforting embrace of a son's loving thoughts. But the gentle rocking of the calm sea casts a merciful spell and slowly eases even these unquiet thoughts. Moonlight falls upon the water, turning it heavy and molten, like mercury laced with silver. My eyes, freighted with so much nocturnal efful-gence, begin to close, and I feel myself drifting off . . .

•

When I awake there is a rosy cummerbund girdling the horizon. However, it is not only the light that has altered. Curious, I engage my other senses, especially that of hearing. I listen, but register nothing out of the ordinary, only the now familiar sound of water lapping against the hull. Nothing else, not even the engine. Oh dear. For some reason we seem to be going nowhere, not to the ends of the earth (or wherever it is that Odysseus wishes to take us), nor even to Capsicum.

Seeing me stir, Odysseus descends from his eyrie. 'No doubt leaving us stranded in the Mediterranean in a boat with no fuel and very little food is all part of the master plan,' he says. 'Unfortunately such a plan is beyond my understanding, so I have come to you seeking guidance. What would you have me do?'

Thus Pumpkin's singular night of glory comes to an unfortunate end.

Communal breakfast in the saloon is necessarily a frugal affair: two fermenting tangerines, and some dry biscuits. When Gumbo complains about the fare on offer, wise-after-the-event Odysseus takes the opportunity to inform the entire company (save the lovebirds) of the newly discovered flaws in my grand design.

'Never mind,' says Gumbo breezily, 'we can always send an SOS to Capsicum.'

'Not without a radio we can't,' says Odysseus. 'The pirates have stripped the vessel of all its valuables, apparently without considering our future needs.'

'Well, this is not a vast ocean but a landlocked sea,' I say. 'We're bound to be spotted soon.'

'Let's hope it's not the pirates who spot us,' says Chickpea.

'Or the Anchovies,' adds Haricot.

Nevertheless, it is impossible to become too fearful on such a breathless and serene day. The sun is in its heaven, and we are afloat on the sea of tranquillity. A Bedu is more likely to find his desert turned to jungle than we are to face a wave. So the consensus survives: all in all, freedom is the better option.

It takes two days of stasis on a stagnant pond before those more accustomed to the semiotics of the city finally realize that the immobile air is not their friend but their mortal enemy. What they need is a breeze, a wind; why, they'd even brave a howling gale were it to blow them to the shore, any shore. They are unspeakably hungry. Hunger and boredom stalk their boat like twin plagues. Only the two lovers, Telemachus and Haidee, remain immune, lost as they are in their own world of carnal delights. A trio of sufferers approaches a fourth, who reclines listlessly in a deckchair. I can tell immediately from their grim expressions that I am an outsider again; no longer a member of the quartet, no longer Good Old Pumpkin.

'Maybe we would have been better off if we had ended our days as slaves,' murmurs Gumbo. 'At least the pirates kept our fleshpots filled, made sure we were never short of bread and meat. Now, thanks to our subtle friend, we are all going to starve to death.'

'You ungrateful bastard,' I say, waving my arms like an upended turtle. 'I don't recall any objections to my plan, either from you or from anyone else. Our imperative was to be free; which we are. Thanks to me.'

'Yes,' says Gumbo, 'free to die.'

Odysseus, who is squatting on the steps that lead to the helm, cannot keep his nose out of the fray.

'Perhaps Mr Pumpkin has another brilliant solution for our new predicament,' he says, 'for which (of course) he bears no special responsibility.'

'The sea is full of fish,' I say.

'We have no bait,' replies Odysseus, 'nor could we ever catch as many as we require.'

'Do you have a better suggestion?' I ask.

'Only the time-honoured one,' replies Odysseus. 'We draw lots, and the loser donates his parts to the pot.'

'It'll never come to that,' I cry. Though I have been wrong before.

Telemachus and Haidee continue to retain the semblance of vitality, feeding as they are off each other's flesh, but the rest of us are fading with alarming rapidity. We are like cadavers that obstinately retain the breath of life; our eyes are rheumy, our skin jaundiced, while our acetate-scented exhalations could blister paint. The one pleasing side effect (as far as I am concerned) is that my bladder has ceased to be a problem, there being hardly any urine to pass. It is, I think, the sixth day of our ordeal. There is still no wind, and even less hope. I await the inevitable end in my favourite deckchair. Odysseus sits on the steps he has made his home. Telemachus and Haidee are isolated in a cabin below. Gumbo, Chickpea, and Haricot are aft, locked in a conspiratorial huddle. Evidently they have decided upon a course of action, for they are staggering midships.

'There is no choice,' says Gumbo. 'If the majority is to survive, one of us must die.'

Silence greets the announcement.

'Since there are no volunteers,' says Chickpea, 'we wish to proceed according to convention.'

The ancient seafarer, who has lost many a companion (though never, so far as I know, eaten one), rises slowly and descends the stairs. He has but one purpose: to secure the life of his child. He pleads for him, urgently requests that the lovers (in recognition of their youth) be excluded from the fatal draw. But his opponents are adamant.

'If they are to benefit,' says one, 'they must also share the risk.'

The debate seems entirely academic to me, since I cannot believe we will ever devour one of our own, but Odysseus clearly possesses a more vivid imagination.

'Oh, you are all childless monsters,' he cries, tormented by the vision of his boy on a spit, 'with no conception of fatherhood.'

That point settled, the proposed meal moves to the next stage: the selection of the main course.

All our names are inscribed on pages ripped hastily

from the yacht's log by Gumbo. The scraps of paper are then folded and dropped into a copper-bottomed saucepan. Although Gumbo shuts his eyes as he reaches inside, I have noted the carnivorous greed in a look directed at me, and fully expect my name to be called. Nor do I intend to rail against the injustice if it is. Despite the privations, I am still the plumpest on board. But my personal fears are unfounded. Gumbo unfolds the paper and reads: 'Telemachus.'

His father's long groan sends a shiver through my kidneys. 'I beg you,' he says, 'take me in his place.'

'Not bloody likely,' replies Gumbo. 'Why settle for mutton when you've been offered lamb?'

'One of us must call the boy,' says Chickpea.

'Let me,' says Odysseus.

And so he summons his only son, whom he loves more than anything in this world or the next; calls him that the unspoilt youth may prolong the lives of such unworthy creatures as Gumbo, Chickpea, and Haricot (not to mention Pumpkin).

'Here I am,' says Telemachus, blinking as he encounters daylight.

Before Odysseus has a chance to respond, Gumbo and his accomplices fall upon the boy and bind him (there being no shortage of rope on a boat).

'Help me, Father!' cries Telemachus.

'Would that I could,' replies Odysseus.

Then Telemachus understands that he is the chosen sacrifice. 'Can no one save me?' he whispers.

'Only the gods,' replies his father.

His lover, meanwhile, has flung herself to the floor (following the precedent set by yours truly), and is hammering her head against the unyielding wood (obviously more convinced than me that we are participating in anything other than a charade). Chickpea steps over her prostrate form on his way to the mess, whence he returns with a knife fit for butchery. A cruel knife none among us has the courage to use. So I am right: the whole business is nothing more than dramaturgy, a substitute for the real thing, a diversion to fool our stomachs. But why are the three heroic epicureans making preparations for a second lottery? 'This seems to be the only way to smoke out a slaughterer,' explains Gumbo, as he impatiently plucks another name from the saucepan. I do not like the sound of this. I like it even less when the name he calls is mine.

'My weapon is the pen, not the knife,' I wail. 'I have no idea how to take another's life.'

'Such ignorance does you credit, Mr Pumpkin,' says Odysseus. 'Those in the know are inhuman beasts, like Polyphemus, who devoured several of my crew. I still weep when I recall how he dashed out their brains and then tore them limb from limb. Touch my boy and you will become the moral equal of a Cyclops.'

Clive Sinclair

'Odysseus over-eggs the pudding,' says Gumbo, pushing me towards the trussed lad. 'All you really need do is make a surgical incision at the wrists and wait as his consciousness ebbs painlessly away. It is true that you will be ending one life, but you will be saving six others. How is that immoral? On the contrary, it is utilitarianism of a high order.' Having delivered me, Gumbo retreats.

The deck is now divided into two unequal parts. In the first (the stern) are the lamb and its slaughterer; in the second are all the remaining interested parties, some willing me on, others unable to watch. But even the most eager witnesses are unaware that a third person has appeared in the stern: the slaughterer's mother.

'So you are not dead after all,' I say.

'Not quite,' she says, 'but as good as. In fact, mistaking you for the Angel of Death, I thought my end was upon me. Tell me, why are you hovering above that frightened boy in such a terrifying manner?'

I explain the dire circumstances. My mother is not impressed.

'Back in Capsicum,' she begins, 'where the Marshal's beleaguered successors are already sacrificing an entire generation of children to save a bankrupt state, I would comfort myself with the thought that my son had been spared the honour of killing and dying for his country. Only to find him aping the crime of those wicked leaders, albeit in miniature. Pumpkin, you have broken a heart that already strains to beat. Yesterday I cursed the doctors who informed me that I had only weeks to live. Now I bless them. Just as I will bless the aeroplanes which drop bombs upon our city. Last night I cowered beneath our impregnable dining table. What for? So that I might survive to see the return of my son, the murderer? Tonight I will pray that a merciful bomb scores a direct hit upon our house and spares me any further agony. Whatever happens, this is certainly our last meeting. Goodbye, my poor boy; as you plunge the knife into that child's breast remember that he too has a mother.' And she is gone, leaving me alone in the world.

Standing over Telemachus with the knife in my hand, I become conscious that its polished blade is no longer flashing, is no longer reflecting the sun. Now a damp wind is licking my cheek like an ingratiating dog. I look around me and note that the sea has curdled; no longer translucent, it more closely resembles a milky-blue emulsion. The sky too has thickened and presses down upon the sea like a suffocating pillow. Overhead it is grey like smoke, but at its farthest reaches it is brown like weak tea.

'Poor Mr Pumpkin,' says Telemachus, 'neither I nor my father will ever blame you for this deed.'

Prompted by his voice, I act without thinking and

sever the ropes that restrain him with a single lacer-
ating stroke.

'If you must eat someone,' I cry, 'eat me.' Whereupon I attempt to plunge the vicious blade deep into
my own belly. But my hand is too unsteady, or my
grip too weak; either way, all I accomplish is the ruin-
ation of my shirt and a pinprick beneath. At the same
time the brown cloud erupts, and sequential forks of
lightning are hurled from the entire length of its purple
underbelly. These celestial fireworks are succeeded
immediately by an earth-shaking crack of thunder.
Gumbo, Chickpea, and Haricot are as apoplectic as the
heavens, but their unkind words are swept away by
an unstoppable gust of wind that takes hold of the
yacht and propels it in a new direction.

Further reflection brings the realization that wind
cannot shift a boat without a sail. In fact we are being
swept along by a strong undersea current, a submarine
reflection of the airborne electricity. Needless to say,
Odysseus sees something more than natural phen-
omena here.

'Poseidon!' he cries, 'if you harm so much as a hair
on my boy's head – especially after what he has just
endured – I'll seek you out, whether you be on the
sandy seabed or atop rocky Mount Olympus. And
when I find you, I'll break your neck. God or no god.'

Whatever its origin the danger is real. As fast as the
yacht is cutting through the turbid sea, the brown

cloud with its legs of fire is travelling even faster. Soon the lightning is almost constant, turning the milky water opalescent and our faces a livid green. Finally, the cloud's dark shadow overwhelms us and we are trapped like flies in the maw of a gigantic bug. We cling to one another helplessly, awaiting terminal enlightenment.

The lightning strikes with such extravagant force that it bisects the twenty-metre boat, flinging the two parts in opposite directions. One part lands to the left of the fast-flowing current, the other to the right. The former bears Odysseus and Telemachus; the latter supports the untouchables. Poor Haidee has somehow been allocated to the wrong group, but there is nothing she can do to remedy the error. A despairing glance tells her that the agitated water between the flotsam and the jetsam cannot be crossed, though communication is just possible over the hubble-bubble.

'Pumpkin,' cries Telemachus, 'can you hear me?'

'So long as you shout,' I reply.

'I place Haidee under your protection,' he yells. 'Make sure those bastards don't eat her.'

'Understood,' I reply, a promise endorsed by a fearsome thunderbolt that makes the very sea vibrate.

'As a matter of fact,' says Gumbo, who is clinging to half-submerged railings beside me, 'I resent being called a bastard. I hope you appreciate that I was not

acting selfishly (after all my name was in the hat too),
but for the greater good.'

'Perhaps "bastard" is too strong,' I say, 'but in my
humble opinion you're presenting symptoms that
suggest you've contracted a nasty bacillus left behind
by the yacht's previous owner.'

'That's not fair,' says Chickpea.

'Not fair at all,' adds Haricot. 'Surely it's better that
six should live at the expense of the seventh, than
that all seven should perish?'

'That's history,' says Haidee. 'Shouldn't we be
applying our collective intelligence to our new predicament?'

'What's to think about?' says Gumbo. 'We can't
cling to these railings for ever. One by one we're bound
to fall asleep, or succumb to hypothermia, or faint
from lack of nourishment; anyway, sooner or later
we're going to let go, and that will be the end of us.'

'Not if you've got something or someone to live for,'
she replies, kicking in the water with her legs. We
follow her example, and the wreckage begins to move
through the water like an ungainly octopus.

Meanwhile (on the opposite bank of the river within
the sea), Odysseus and Telemachus propel their raft
in a similar fashion, and all afternoon we run on parallel courses, waving encouragement across the great
divide. When darkness comes and covers the face of
the waters, Haidee shouts out the name of her lover,

and is buoyed to hear her own name returned. For hour after hour the call and respond continues, until a strong wind arises and puts an end to the duet. Undaunted, Haidee's relentless solo lasts the remainder of the night: 'Telemachus, Telemachus . . .' By dawn our erstwhile companions are no longer visible. Instead we can see huge rollers, and beyond them an island whose mountains penetrate the clouds. The clouds themselves, touched by the radiance of the rising sun, are as purple as the late Marshal's nose (a bulbous object, grouted throughout with broken blood vessels, to which I had always turned a blind eye). They provide a flattering backing for a glittering rainbow which arches above the island. Its end is in a dense forest whose painted leaves would make the most ostentatious autumnal display seem spinsterish.

'Could there be a better omen than that?' I gasp. 'Our troubles must surely be at an end.'

Between them the heavyweight breakers and the sabre-toothed rocks do their best to prove me wrong. Especially when our fragile support is thrown against the latter by the former and instantly reduced to driftwood. We are tossed like dice in the palm of the sea-god and cast mercifully into the path of a spent wave, which deposits us naked upon the terracotta shore. Haidee lies supine and motionless, fully exposed to all senses and elements. I prepare to defend her honour against the hand of Gumbo & Co., but immediately recognize that their libidos are as frail as their other parts.

'Now what?' moans Gumbo, squatting head on knees like an Inca mummy.

'First we cover what only Telemachus has the right to see,' I say, 'then I suggest we investigate the source of the smoke that is rising above those oaks.'

So we fashion Haidee a bikini out of the soft fronds of giant ferns, and hide our privates as best we can. The unconscious girl awakens and, like dawn, blushes red when she deduces the identity of her tailors. Reassured that we have not challenged her lover's monopoly, she agrees to accompany us across the sand and into the forest, which extends almost to the sea. No sooner do we enter it than the noises begin: roaring that sounds as if it emanates from angry lions, bear-like snorting, and the tragic howling that is exclusive to wolves.

'It seems possible that we have come full circle,' I say, 'and ended up almost where we began, on the Marshal's private isle.'

'What if those animals are as hungry as we are?' asks Chickpea.

'We'll know the answer to that one soon enough,' replies Haricot, as we are suddenly surprised by a menagerie of carnivores. But they do not behave as such; rather they act the part of lost souls who happen to be wearing the countenances and skins of wild beasts. The expressions on those faces are of frustration and longing, as if they want nothing more than to question us and obtain news of the world outside the animal kingdom.

The path we are following rises steeply through the dense arboretum, overpopulated with cork and oak, and finally peters out in a lush upland meadow, at the far end of which stands a dazzling palace clad in white marble. Resinous smoke rises from its central yard, carrying the aroma of pine and roasting lamb. Our appetites roused beyond recall and, already anticipating the taste of slightly charred meat, we hurry towards the source of so much promise, only to have our way constantly barred by the strangely mannered animals. Despite their persistent muzzling we achieve our goal and are instantly enchanted by the sweet song of an unknown female within.

'We can't stop now,' says Gumbo, grasping the door-knocker (itself shaped like a clenched hand) and banging it hard. Almost at once the portal opens to reveal a woman of divine beauty so radiant that it hurts the eyes to look upon her. The wild beasts are even more afflicted, instantly retreating to the thickets whence they came. She looks at us quizzically, but there is no need for any to speak; our appearance is a sufficiently eloquent advocate of our plight. 'My poor friends,' she croons, 'please enter. It will be my pleasure to clothe and feed you.'

She leads us down a staircase cut through solid rock, each step bracketed by a pair of amphorae, and through an atrium open to the sky. Beyond that is the main body of the palace. Our hostess invites us to enter its dining room, a vast space flooded with natural light, thanks to the fact that one of its walls is constructed entirely of glass. Looking out of these windows we can see that the palace is built on the edge of a perpendicular cliff. Far below us are the cruel rocks that shredded the remnant of our craft, and all around is the roiling sea that we have (by some miracle) safely crossed.

'What is the name of this place?' I suddenly think to ask. But our hostess does not hear my question, or chooses to ignore it.

'While my kitchen staff prepare your meal,' she says, 'I shall order other servants to bring you robes, so that you will feel more comfortable when you dine. After that you will have plenty of time to bathe and sleep.'

'Who do you think she is?' asks Gumbo, as soon as our benefactress is elsewhere.

'Probably one of the Marshal's mistresses,' I reply, all the more convinced that I have – too late, too late – finally reached the place where I would have got my scoop, the exclusive interview with the Marshal that would have turned me from a hack into an ace reporter. The Isle of Transformations.

The subject of our speculations, the Lady of the Isle, returns accompanied by two ebony-skinned hand-maidens, both of whom are bearing brightly coloured robes made of cloth from Paprika.

'Please put them on and be seated,' says our glorious hostess, 'and then I will listen to your story while you eat.'

Clearly moved by the narrative of our tribulations, our hostess feeds us small portions of cheese, honey, barley, and the eagerly awaited lamb (which is embell-ished with apricots and almonds). Also available is a large platter of local fungi, which Haidee will not touch, but which the rest of us devour with gusto; prominent amid this autumnal harvest are pinkish mushrooms smelling of coconut, red caps that scorch the tongue, more familiar morels tasting of new-baked bread, and (best of all) sweet and nutty truffles. Mean-while our benefactress pours generous amounts of red wine into silver goblets, at the same time as advising us to quaff with caution. Before long our heads are dropping as sleep overpowers our bodies, whereupon our ever attentive hostess summons a smiling servant who shows us to our separate rooms, each of which is cooled by sea breezes and suffused with the scent of lavender and other potent soporifics. What bliss it is to surrender my senses on a soft divan beneath a cotton quilt filled with feathers. I dream that the Lady of the Isle enters my quarters and gently touches me

on the shoulder with her wand; a gesture that makes
me feel even more comfortable.

It is still night when I awaken (or appear to
awaken), and the darkness does nothing to assist my
orientation. Clearly I have fallen from my bed, for I
am stiff and cold and resting on a pallet of straw. Gone
too is the sweet breath of incense; in its place is the
intestinal stench of the farmyard.

No wonder: the place is full of swine. One of them,
a bristling brute with an all-over crew cut, long snout,
and curved tusks is actually swaggering towards my
stall. It takes one look at me and then, to my amazement, says: 'Not another fucking pig. Where the hell
is everyone else?' Not only does the pig speak, it speaks
in a voice that I recognize, a voice that is indubitably
Gumbo's. Since porkers possess neither the ear nor the
vocal talents of parrots, my best guess is that the poor
fellow has been swallowed whole.

'Don't panic, Gumbo,' I say, confident that the
maneater won't have room for seconds, 'we'll open
that monster's belly and have you out in next to no
time.'

The creature totters backwards, as though
recovering from a blow. 'Pumpkin,' it grunts, 'if I didn't
know that it was impossible, I'd say that you had
evolved overnight, and that Pumpkin Mark 2 was a
pig.'

At which point I cotton on to the fact that I am the

butt of one of Gumbo's practical jokes, and that he must be throwing his voice from the far side of the sty. I assume that Chickpea and Haricot are beside him and beside themselves, all crouching behind a bale of hay.

'I had no idea you were such a talented ventriloquist,' I say. 'For a moment you had me believing that you really were inside that ugly brute. But the joke's over, so own up and tell me where you're hiding.'

The creature approaches me again, coming so close that I can smell its musty breath. 'Are you crazy, Pumpkin,' it says. 'I'm standing right in front of you.'

'The only thing in front of me is a hog,' I say.

It groans. 'So what has happened to you has happened to me too,' it says.

'Nothing has happened to me,' I insist.

As I speak I am suddenly overcome by an undeniable urge to pee. To my astonishment I rise and empty my bladder on to my bedding without a second thought. It simply gushes forth. As I look down at the wet straw I observe that my nose has been reshaped and greatly extended so that it more closely resembles a snout. Also my teeth now protrude quite noticeably from my mouth. My first impulse is to explore these changes with my right hand, but it refuses to budge. And that is when I learn that I am no longer bipedal;

I am a quadruped with dainty trotters in place of hands and feet.

'I think I know what's going on, Gumbo,' I say, trying to remain reasonable. 'You've somehow strayed into my dream, though nightmare might be a better word. Now go back to your bed, and let me sleep on in mine.'

There is a rustle in the straw behind me, from where a pink gilt emerges. 'Am I in your dream too?'

The voice is unmistakable. 'Haidee?' I say.

'The same,' she replies miserably.

Soon Chickpea and Haricot appear, in similar livery. This is no dream after all, but the beginning of my life as a pig. (If only my father were alive to see me. Maybe he would love me now.)

•

It is a moot point as to whether my condition would be more bearable if my mind had been transformed along with my body, but since it wasn't I continue to regard myself as a man imprisoned within the form of a pig. True, this is somewhat confining, but at least I have the companionship of like-minded boars, whereas poor Haidee is kept in splendid isolation as the only sow. This isolation is obviously beginning to tell upon her, because she is suddenly off her food (or so a stockman observed yesterday), and is making uncharacteristic efforts to seek out our company.

Although we can communicate amongst ourselves, our speech means nothing to the aforementioned stockman who sees to our diurnal and nocturnal needs, which are not great: clean straw, water, and acorns. But when it comes to Haidee he is more like a suitor, lavishing attention upon her, paying particular heed to the most intimate parts of her body. I am astounded that she permits such liberties, and am even more distressed to see her eventually court them. It is the stockman's custom to squeeze her shoulder when he first enters her stall. Today she responds by standing and presenting herself to him in a way that would make Telemachus jealous (even in her present state).

'Her vulva's as red as a blood orange, and her clit's as big as a grape,' observes the stockman. 'What do these signs tell you?'

'That the girl's hot to trot,' replies his apprentice.

'Precisely,' replies his boss. 'Now which of those fine fellows is going to be the lucky boar?'

'Why not the fat one?' says his apprentice cheerfully.

That very afternoon I am conducted to Haidee's stall, where I am expected to do my duty and impregnate her.

'What happens if he's a reluctant groom?' asks the apprentice *en route*.

'No problem,' replies the stockman, 'we'll just shove

an electrode up his rectum. That has never yet failed
to kick-start the action.'

How I wish that I had not understood a single word
of their exchange. It's not nice to know that if I behave
like a mensch and refuse to betray my friend, I'll be
buggered with a hot poker.

'Oestrus is so humiliating,' says Haidee, as soon as
we are left alone. 'I don't want you anywhere near
me, but at the same time my cunt is so wet it's embar-
rassing. I suppose I'll blub like a deflowered virgin if
you fuck me, but I'm certain I'll scream if you don't.'
Sure enough she emits a series of high-pitched grunts.
'Pumpkin, do me a favour, get on my back and stick
your dick in me.'

'How can I?' I say (trying to ignore the consequences of my masochistic chivalry). 'I gave my word
to Telemachus that I would protect you come what
may.'

'Do you think I have forgotten Telemachus and that
promise (though I doubt whether "come what may"
included transformation into a sow)?' she says. 'But
just now my pig's body is stronger than my woman's
mind, and it wants me in the gutter. So get pumping,
Pumpkin.'

I am about to utter some more high-minded sentiments when I get a whiff of the pheromones being
churned out by her hyperactive reproductive organs,
and I'm also lost to reason and decency. I nuzzle her

overripe opening, then unceremoniously piss on the straw. What next? Needless to say, I've never fucked a pig before, but somehow my body knows exactly what to do. I mount Haidee from the rear and, digging my front trotters into her flanks, guide my erect member home. Without forethought I find myself biting the loose flesh at the base of her neck.

'I'm not hurting you, am I?' I gasp.

'What do you think?' moans Haidee, before adding: 'Harder! Do it harder, you fat pig!'

Does she want me to bite harder, or to push harder? To be on the safe side I do both. Not that I have any choice when it comes to the latter. It's as though my whole body is trying to enter Haidee prick first. Nor is she exactly passive. While her human half weeps for shame at this abject capitulation to her bestial instincts, her animal half simultaneously squeals like a stuck pig. Meanwhile my hips seem to have developed a mind of their own, and my back legs are trembling with about-to-be-fulfilled desire. Unfortunately, just as my muscles are tensing for the final thrust, my trotters lose their purchase on a floor made slippery by my earlier discharge, and they skitter backwards with frightening velocity, causing me to fall flat on my face, and (incidentally) to commit the sin of Onan.

Next morning Gumbo is invited to cover Haidee. Judging by the squeaks and squeals of carnal satisfaction he is evidently more successful than his predecessor.

'That wasn't at all bad,' he announces as he struts back. 'True, she was a pig, but she was on fire, and a fuck's a fuck.'

Chickpea and Haricot are not ignored, getting their turns on the morrow. Within days it is clear to all that Haidee is pregnant. Thereafter she is mollycoddled by the stockman and his lad, while we are left alone to forage on the forest floor for fungi or fallen acorns. Precisely three months, three weeks, and three days after the event (that is to say, in deep mid-winter) she gives birth to a litter of eight. An easy time she has of it, the newborns popping out like wet soap from a fist. The only other birth I have attended – my own – was (according to the chief witness) a very different matter, me being such a reluctant debutant, and enormous to boot. Given the pain I caused her (said my mother), it's a small miracle she ever managed to forgive me, and an even greater one that she found it in her heart to love me. Motherhood does that to you (said my canny mater).

It certainly does something to Haidee; above all, it brings her human and animal parts into closer harmony. In her eyes those creatures constantly worrying her udders are neither man nor beast but simply her babies (though they look one hundred per cent porcine to me). Fatherhood is more problematic.

Despite the fact that their mother has given each of the new arrivals a name, none of the potential sires either uses or chooses to remember a single one of them. At least I have coitus interruptus to justify my lack of paternal interest. I am absolutely certain that I am not the father. All Gumbo, Chickpea, and Haricot can offer as an excuse is uncertainty, though they can be sure that one of their number is certainly the sperm donor supreme. Anyway, the indifferent boars continue to frequent the forest, leaving Haidee reclining on her side contentedly suckling the piglets, the very image of maternity. This happy state continues for three weeks. On the twenty-second day, however, the piglets are removed from their mother with many a sad little oink. For her part Haidee wails like a tragedienne, but there is little she can do once confined to her sty except fling herself against the wicket. 'Don't worry, old girl,' says the stockman, 'you'll be carrying another litter within the week.'

A sort of madness overtakes Haidee, and she becomes obsessed with the idea that her progeny await vivisection in an annex of the palace. When asked for evidence she offers only 'a mother's intuition'. Alas, even if wrong, she cannot be far off the mark; no one imagines that the infants have been enrolled at the local kindergarten. So we sympathize with her constant lamentation, which doesn't stop it driving us crazy. As a consequence, we try to keep our distance.

No hardship, in truth; I've started to enjoy these outings with the lads, now that I'm able to piss uninhibitedly in the woods whenever I feel like it, and shit without having to worry whether extra-soft toilet tissue is to hand.

'She's completely lost all sense of proportion,' remarks Gumbo sagely as we stroll home, our bellies distended with acorns, hob-nuts, and wind. 'I mean, the future for piglets has never exactly been rosy. The best they can ever hope for is a picturesque end, roasting whole on a spit.'

'Veneered with marinades,' adds Chickpea.

'Not forgetting the red apple in the mouth,' says Haricot, giving the picture a final touch.

It doesn't seem to cross any of their minds that the piggy-in-the-middle could well be flesh of their flesh. I recall, with a shudder, our earlier flirtation with cannibalism. How long ago was that?

When we reach the sty we discover, to our surprise, that Haidee has abandoned hysteria. Instead of a febrile drama queen, there's an ice maiden, too obviously under control. It is the calm before the storm. The storm breaks at midnight, when Haidee's voice (rather than thunder) summons me from the land of nod.

'I've been listening to my fucking biological clock ticking all night,' she says, 'and I don't like what it's been telling me. I don't like it, but I know it's what's what. I know that (like it or not) I'll be presenting my rump to you and your friends again in a matter of days. It's what sows do; they get fucked, and they farrow. When the second litter comes, I'll no longer have time to fret about the first. So I need to find out what's happening to those innocents right now. Don't look so alarmed, Pumpkin. All I'm asking of you is to get me out of here.'

'Then what will you do?' I enquire.

'Break into the palace,' she replies.

'How?' I ask.

'With consummate ease,' she says. 'Do you remember the dining room, the one that felt as if it were floating on air?'

'Of course.'

'Well,' she continues, 'I happened to notice that there was actually a lip of land between it and the sea; a trim moustache of grass. With that in mind, I intend to skirt the perimeter of the compound and gain entry via one of the dining room's many windows. It's a hot night, and some are sure to be ajar.'

'Spoken like Captain Mandragora's daughter,' I say, 'but aren't you forgetting that you're presently a pig, and that pigs are not built to leap around like cat burglars.'

I can see that I am wasting my breath, and that Haidee is determined to carry out her half-baked plan, which contains no provision for what to do in the unlikely event of discovering the missing links. My own mother would be just as obstinate if her son were in danger, I'm sure. Sick as she is, hasn't she been with me in spirit – always ready with good advice – until her strength finally ran out?

'If you have a better idea, Pumpkin,' says Haidee, growing impatient, 'I'd be glad to hear it. Otherwise, I'd be obliged if you would be so kind as to slip my bolt with your snout.'

What can I do but obey? What can I do – given my promise to Telemachus – but accompany her on her mission impossible?

The bright moon illuminates our path, and we step out as daintily as two swine can. It takes only a couple of minutes to reach the palace's front gate, flanked tonight by a pair of flaming torches.

'Looks like she's throwing a party,' I observe, and immediately find myself fighting the conviction that suckling pig is on the menu within.

We circumnavigate the building without incident, then begin to edge our way along its rear. Haidee is right: there is a narrow shelf between the wall and empty space, a very narrow shelf. It is dark, of course, but I recall without difficulty the enormity of the drop and the severity of the punishment awaiting pigs who think they can fly. Having full confidence in my inability, I ensure that my left flank remains in contact with the building at all times. Haidee, however, moves with the grace of a mountain pig, if such a thing exists.

Flickering candles make it obvious that the dining room is occupied by partygoers (albeit very quiet ones). It is our intention to wait patiently until the wicks are snuffed, but after an hour curiosity gets the better of us and we risk a peep through the glass. Our enchanting hostess is present, of course (incidentally, I realized her true identity only when it was too late; not the Marshal's mistress, but a far more ancient *femme fatale*, none other than Circe herself). In fact she only has two guests, and I know them both immediately (although the younger has his back to the window): Odysseus and Telemachus.

'My love,' gasps Haidee, 'my love still lives.'

The poor girl is torn between the desire to save her lover from the witch's vindictive magic, and the fear that he might recognize his saviour and turn from her in revulsion.

'Don't worry on their account,' I whisper. 'Odysseus knows the score.'

'Do my eyes deceive me,' he says, 'or are there two pigs staring at us?'

'Perhaps they are the proud parents of this little graduate,' Circe says, cutting some more slices from the tender hock of the anticipated sacrifice.

Convinced now that her precious babes have all been butchered, and tantalized by the proximity of her untouchable lover, Haidee steps back from the window, turns, and leaps towards the precipice. She is swifter than me, but I have foreseen her suicidal gesture, and use my greater bulk to divert her trajectory.

'You must not give up hope,' I say.

'Why not?' cries Haidee.

'Because this is not how the story ends,' I say.

'Well, things certainly can't get any worse,' she concedes.

•

The stockman takes one look at Haidee's genitalia and says: 'Not tonight, Josephine.' Nonetheless, she is locked in her sty for her own protection (lest any of the boars tries to mount her prematurely). Knowing her to be safe from harm (and self-harm), I head off for the woods alone, anxious to root out some truffles I got wind of yesterday when I spotted (out of the corner of my eye) a rash of yellow flies hovering over a particular plot of land. The others (less concerned for Haidee's welfare) wouldn't wait and departed without me, which is their loss; now I won't have to share any of my buried treasure. The anticipation of this secret pleasure in store keeps diverting my mind from that other big question: how to make our plight known to Odysseus? I decide to worry about that one after lunch, and proceed directly through the budding brambles and broom to a cluster of ancient oaks, among whose roots the bulbous truffles lie. Pausing where the flies freckle the air, I lower my neck and sniff a heady cocktail of the putrid and the decaying. So intent am I on isolating the single molecule that will pinpoint the hiding place of the exclusive fungi that I remain deaf and blind to all else. That is until my senses are all but overwhelmed by the sickly scent of wild cyclamen.

Looking around I see that a couple is reclining upon a bed of the stuff, the rabbit-eared blooms obviously cajoled into an early showing by the sweet-talk of a false spring. Let's hope Odysseus is made of sterner stuff, for Circe's honey-trap looks mighty hard to resist (even to me, a hog).

'About a month ago I was visited by a dream,' I hear her say, 'a dream or a vision. Anyway, I saw two wings, the wings of a great white bird. Perhaps an albatross. I cannot say for sure because the bird had no body. All that remained of it were those magnificent wings, with their raw and bloody stumps. But it was not a sad vision. Oh no. Those wings were alive. And they were aloft, gliding across a sky of the deepest blue. I knew at once what the dream meant: that Odysseus or Oudeis – that is, Nobody – would soon be returning to me. That my long, long wait would be over.' She looks enticingly at her once and (she hopes) future paramour.

'Come,' she says, patting the bank beside her, 'sit a little closer.'

Odysseus obliges, the old fool.

'Expecting your arrival daily I kept a vigil in my palace,' she says, 'watching the endless sea for a sail. Eventually my patience was rewarded; the small boat docked and a ruddy-bearded sailor disembarked with his son. I knew immediately that the sailor was you. And hope whispered to my heart: "Beat the drum, this time he will surely stay." But experience cautioned: "He is on a quest; you could not stop him from returning to his wife on the first occasion, nor will you succeed on the second." I recognized wisdom in the words of experience and, seeing that you were already on the path to my palace, peeled off my lips so that I would not be tempted to kiss you. Then I bit off my tongue so that I would not be able to say, "I love you." When I watched you enter the forest, I threw away my arms so that I would not be able to wrap them around you. By the time you crossed the meadow my legs were no longer mine. Finally, as you knocked on my door, I scooped out my cunt so that I would not be able to pleasure you. After all that I was amazed when you greeted me quite normally and did not see anything amiss in the bleeding torso who welcomed you.'

Surely this is my cue to intervene; to save him, if not myself. Following the example of the wild beasts we encountered on our approach to the palace, I enter the clearing and unashamedly fawn upon Odysseus. It did me no good with the Marshal (when I looked like a human, but behaved like a dog), and it does me no good now; Circe simply brushes me aside.

'What's the meaning of this, Circe,' says Odysseus, 'are you up to your old tricks?'

I nod my head vigorously, like a grotesque in a pantomime, but alas Odysseus only has eyes for his companion.

'You do me an injustice, old friend,' she says, 'as you will hear.'

'I'm all ears,' he replies.

'Knowing that you were on your way,' she says, 'I immediately disposed of my current amour.'

Odysseus looks straight at me: 'Tell me that isn't him,' he says.

'Of course it isn't,' says Circe sharply, 'although there is a connection. If you want to check, he's head of surgery at the paediatric hospital on the other side of the island. Anyway, his dream was to graft bespoke organs from pig to man, but he could see no way of overcoming the risk of unknown retroviruses. So he came to me, the acknowledged expert on xenotransplantation. At first I was reluctant to assist, knowing how my talents have been misrepresented before, but he was a persistent fellow, and on our first date introduced me to the residents of his surgical ward: some twenty children dying for want of a kidney or a heart. I was persuaded, quickly acquired four boars and a sow, did this and that with their genes, and let nature take its course. This sycophant is one of those pioneers, the pig-in-a-million destined to provide my ex-lover with his raw material. The first operations were performed last week. A score or more young children, who would otherwise be dead, are now looking forward to a new life. Oh, Odysseus, if only you could have seen the tears of the grateful parents (which were sweeter to me than ambrosia), you would have fallen in love with me on the spot.'

The words have their desired effect upon their primary listener, but they also cause me to experience unexpected pain on behalf of a parent at the other end of the food chain. It seems that Haidee was dead right when it came to predicting the fate of her own. Trust a mother to know. But would it do her any good to learn that her fears were justified? It is a difficult question, but nothing compared with the continuing problem of communicating with Odysseus. Once again I attempt to lick his cheek and hand. Once more Circe dismisses me, giving me the distinct impression that if I am not more retiring I risk being turned to stone.

'I never thought that a goddess could be jealous of a swine,' says Circe with a voluptuous sigh, 'but you have just permitted that creature liberties I dare not take. Do not look so aghast, Odysseus, I have determined to embarrass neither myself nor you. So (before I am overcome by an irresistible urge to touch) let us go straight back to the palace.'

'Good idea,' he says, rising to his feet. 'Telemachus must be wondering what's happened to me.'

'Not a bloody thing,' says Circe.

Only after they have returned whence they came do I wonder how she was able to perform the extraordinary feat of removing her cunt without any hands.

Anyway, the organ must have grown back during the night because next time I see the couple Odysseus is pumping his all into it. Although familiar with the penalties available for seeing a goddess in the altogether, I cannot help but watch her in amorous action. Her body hardly moves at all, merely quivers gently like a leaf in a breeze, and when Odysseus finishes she simply coos like a dove. Afterwards she says to Odysseus: 'It's cruel to leave me so soon.'

'I'm not going anywhere,' he says, stroking her cheek.

'Yes you are,' she says. 'I only have to look in your eyes to see that you're already vanishing, withdrawing like an octopus into its undersea cave. I do not dispute that your body is here, but your mind is already elsewhere, far away from here.'

'I am sorry,' says Odysseus, 'but I cannot forget the duty I owe to Penelope. She waited for me to come home all those years. And now she is having to wait again. It isn't fair.'

'Nor is what you have just done fair to me,' says Circe. 'How do you think it feels to know you've been fucked by a man who won't remember you tomorrow? Your wife is the one who is dead, but I feel like the ghost. And maybe that is how it should be. She certainly has more right to be with you than I have, who really has no right to you at all, and even less to happiness (as my nightmares constantly remind me). Only last night I dreamed that I was a sea cow or manatee, swimming through cloudy waters towards a man shedding light. You were the man, of course, and paddle as I might I couldn't reach you. Why was I a manatee? Because its name accounts for my failure, being (like me) just a little short of humanity. Nor do I have any cause for complaint; unhappiness is my just dessert.'

'Just dessert for what?' asks Odysseus.

'I killed my first husband,' replies Circe.

'Killed as in murdered?' asks Odysseus.

'Not quite,' replies Circe. 'I drove him to death because I didn't reciprocate his love sufficiently.'

'You mean he killed himself?' asks Odysseus.

'As good as,' replies Circe. 'He kept taking foolish risks, which suggests to me that he didn't care whether he lived or died. Eventually he took one risk too many.'

'Even so, that was a long time ago,' says Odysseus.

'My husband was not the last man who suffered on my account,' says Circe. 'The world is full of my discarded suitors, who live out their lives in more appropriate shapes. Few men have ever left here unaltered. One of them being the only man I cannot have. Alas, time has done to him what I could not. It has stolen his better half and turned him into a grieving widower.'

Circe sits up and cradles her lover's hands within her own.

'Listen, Odysseus,' she whispers, 'I love you so much that if it were within my power I would gladly enter the gates of Hades and, finding your wife's shade, say: "I am here to take your place." If I close my eyes I can easily picture her walking up the steep path towards the light. I can even imagine her outfit: a purple skirt, and a white top. As we go our opposite ways, I will reach out and briefly touch her. And then, imagining your reunion, I will descend into the lower depths with joy.'

Odysseus says: 'Look into my eyes. Am I here now?'

'You are here now,' says Circe.

He reaches into the golden triangle between her legs. Circe's initial response is breathless excitement, but after a while she begins to moan, 'No, no, no . . .,' in a fluttery voice.

Odysseus immediately removes his finger and says, 'Do you really want me to stop?'

And she says: 'I'm not sure.'

And he says: 'You sounded pretty certain just now.'

And she says: 'Don't you know that when a woman says "no", she often means "yes"?'

And Odysseus says: 'So you want me to continue?'

And she says: 'See what happens.'

So Odysseus returns to the task in hand. Again she says: 'No, no, no . . .,' adding, 'not yet, not yet.'

This time Odysseus ignores her denials. Holding her tightly he works on her clitoris until her 'no, no, no . . .' ceases, and she cedes control of her body.

She cries: 'Do you want me to come?'

He says: 'Yes.'

She says: 'I want to come in your hand.' Then she moves like a birch in a hurricane, shaking until she is entirely uprooted. Weeping, she says: 'Odysseus, I believe you've just raped me.'

'But you told me that when you said "no", you really meant "yes",' he protests.

'Ah,' she says, 'but sometimes when I say "no", I mean "no".'

'Are you telling me you didn't enjoy the experience?' he asks.

'I enjoyed it very much,' she replies. 'In fact it was the first time a man has ever made me come.'

He says: 'That can't be true.'

Circe says: 'Don't forget I'm a goddess, and most men are happy enough with what I permit them. Even you, once upon a time. Obviously you have learned much in the intervening years. Enough to risk demanding more of a goddess. Consequently you alone have seen me in so vulnerable a state, and – like it or not – have added me to your list of dependants.'

'I'm aware of that,' says Odysseus, kissing her breasts.

Circe shivers, but not only with pleasure. 'Shall we go back soon,' she says, 'it's getting chilly.'

•

It's an even colder morning, and we all opt for the warmth of the sty rather than face the rigours of a gale from the north. We're still dozing on our mattresses of straw when the stockman arrives to assess Haidee's readiness.

'The wind out there is probably stiffer than any of this lot,' says the stockman to his apprentice. 'Little wonder she doesn't want to know.'

As soon as the stockman has departed, Gumbo rushes to the gate in order to make faces behind the back of the blackguard who has queried his manhood (if 'manhood' is still the appropriate epithet). We cheer him on, until he suddenly goes all serious. 'I think you'd all better take a look,' he says, pointing to a familiar man and a boy striding across the courtyard in our direction.

It seems that I am the only one to greet our

discovery by Odysseus and Telemachus with unambiguous gratitude. Of course I appreciate why Haidee feels the need to bury her face in her bedding, but don't really understand why Gumbo's hocks have started to tremble so alarmingly.

'What's eating you?' I enquire.

'Nothing's eating me,' he replies. 'It's what we wanted to eat that's the problem. Do you think the old man's really forgiven us for trying to barbecue his son and heir?'

'We'll soon find out,' I say cheerfully (wondering how the canny sleuths managed to track us down). Except that they aren't coming to see us after all. It is quickly apparent that the purpose of their excursion is to put some distance between the pair of them and the palace. Self-righteous Telemachus is apparently furious with his father.

'What do you mean "you want to stay here a little longer"? How much is a "little longer"?' he fumes. 'What will your daughter-in-law – the one you forswore rest to find – do in the meantime? Or are you prepared to abandon her to her fate, however terrible that might be? Not to mention your wife, my mother. Have you so easily forgotten the purpose of our journey, why we set out in the first place? Or have you persuaded yourself that it's all right to tarry here pleasuring yourself with that whore, because time has no meaning in Hades; and so it matters not whether

Penelope waits a further five, ten, or fifteen years for the only man she has ever loved?'

Odysseus, who is leaning against the rough-hewn door of our sty, holds his tongue, letting intemperate youth have its say. It's an ill wind, I think; his fall is bound to improve our chances of enlisting his help.

'Father,' continues Telemachus, 'you already have the love of a good woman, so why did you have to succumb to another's wiles? You are old and respected, and yet when presented with temptation you showed as much self-restraint as one of those stinking hogs, who know only instinct, and nothing of duty.'

'Bloody cheek,' snorts Gumbo.

Haidee maintains her silence, but I can see that the words have stabbed her to the heart; hot tears are spilling from her piggy eyes and rolling down her puff-pastry cheeks. 'Oh, Pumpkin,' she weeps, 'if that boy only knew how much will power I am exercising in order to delay oestrus. But try as I might I cannot postpone it for ever. If it doesn't happen today, then it will certainly happen tomorrow.'

She pauses to regain her composure. Outside, the wind continues at full cry, as does Telemachus.

'How wrong I was when I said that things couldn't get any worse!' continues Haidee. 'Here's one way they could: I'm being serviced by Gumbo, and (despite myself) enjoying every minute, when guess who walks by. Believe me, Pumpkin, if Telemachus were to catch me *in flagrante delicto* with a pig I should never be able to live with the shame of it.'

Time, it seems, is not on our side after all. On the contrary, it is our enemy. To sum up: if I am not able to make our plight known to Odysseus in the next day or so, Haidee will most likely kill herself.

And so next morning's blizzard is a novelty verging on the miraculous. No one alive has seen snow fall on Circe's isle. Within minutes the ground has become false spring's icy shroud. Telemachus, captivated by the world's new innocence, rushes from the palace and dances for joy, his ecstatic cries breaking Haidee's heart anew. Odysseus follows and, smiling to see his boy so carefree again, makes a snowball and picks a fight. Inspired by the runes his fingers scrape in the snow, the class idiot has a brainwave. Rousing Gumbo, Chickpea, and Haricot, I insist that they follow me. As I lead them at a trot through the snow towards Odysseus, I come over all sergeant-majorish and order them to stop bellyaching about chilblains and listen to my simple instructions. Reaching our erstwhile companion, we stand accordingly in formation and start to write on the virgin snow like a team of synchronized pissers. I trace the letter 'H'. Gumbo produces 'E', Chickpea 'L', and Haricot 'P'. It takes the old sea-dog but a nanosecond to work out what has happened to us (he has, don't forget, seen it all before).

'Is it really you, Pumpkin?' he cries. 'And the others, I suppose, are Gumbo, Chickpea, and Haricot?'

I grunt affirmatively (or so I hope).

'But what of my son's wife,' he adds, 'what of Haidee? Does she live? Where is she? Is she kept somewhere in the palace?' He pauses. 'Why do you not respond?' Then the penny drops. 'Not, surely, with you in the sty?' For once I am thankful that I cannot speak. 'Go back there,' says Odysseus. 'Meanwhile I have a bone to pick with that two-faced bitch. Do not fear; your exile from humanity is almost at an end.'

And so it comes to pass at midnight that Odysseus brings Circe to the sty. The latter is wearing a loose shift of thin cotton, which can barely contain the golden allure of her flesh. No cuts or bruises are visible. Her eyes, however, are red.

'Put yourself in my shoes,' says the goddess, obviously still keen upon justifying her actions to a mere mortal (forget the porcines). 'Four dishevelled mendicants and a notorious cut-throat's daughter show up out of the blue, bearing the heart-stopping news that the love of my life is finally within touching distance,' — though the girl neglects to mention that his son is the love of her life. '— meanwhile, children are continuing to die for want of scientific know-how. All I need do to save those children, and (maybe, just maybe) win my approaching lover's admiration in the process, is to transform those outlaws into a breeding herd of swine. No one else knows they are alive, let alone here. What would you do? Speaking for myself, I give in to temptation. Then when you tell me that that the girl was your boy's new bride – in a manner of speaking – my heart sinks, but it's already too late. There are two dozen kids at least whose lives depend upon her next litter. So the lies begin.'

'Next litter?' echoes Odysseus.

'I told you,' says Circe, 'the programme has already started.'

'Does that mean what I think it means?' he asks.

Circe nods.

'One thing is certain,' says Odysseus, 'Telemachus must never know that he is the stepfather of pigs.'

'So what would you have me do?' asks Circe.

'For a start, you must restore Haidee to her original state,' replies Odysseus, 'then honest Pumpkin, who did me a great service. As to the others – who were swine even when dressed up as human beings – let them stay as pigs.'

Hearing this judgement Gumbo, Chickpea, and Haricot approach the speaker as supplicants, the bristles on their snouts wet with tears. But Odysseus remains unmoved by their anguished whinnies.

'What have you three got to blub about?' he demands. 'Your lives – formerly worthless – suddenly have purpose. You have become VIPs – Very Important Pigs – the *sine qua non* of a successful medical experiment. Surely that's a step up from being a cog in the conspiracy that conned a generation into believing that its leader was a great man? You'll recall that we experienced his legacy at Pomodoro. Now instead of poisoning young minds you have become instrumental in robbing death of youthful victims.' So saying, Odysseus scatters the lachrymose porkers with kicks up the backside. 'Ungrateful swine,' he cries. 'Instead of this repellent display of self-pity, you should be on your knees thanking Circe.'

'If you think my husbandry is so priceless, how come you are prepared to leave me short of a sow?' wonders Circe.

'That is not my intention,' replies Odysseus. 'I am almost convinced that these transformations were not performed for the sake of mischief, but done to capture my heart, and (incidentally) do good. But (knowing your record) some doubt still lingers. Especially since the deeds have cost you nothing. If you really want me to believe in your love, you must give me a greater proof. Take Haidee's place.'

Divine Circe does not flinch. 'If that's what you require,' she says, 'then I shall do it without protest. I was not lying when I said I would gladly exchange places with your wife, and I am not bluffing now. Even when I hoped against hope that you would volunteer to remain here with me, I always knew in my heart that your journey, once begun, would have to be completed. How else to explain yesterday's strange purchase? Before making my weekly visit to the paediatric hospital I toured the adjacent market, intending to buy some amusements for the small patients. Immediately my eye was attracted to a stall that was more a shrine to the tortoiseshell comb. The combs were exquisite: mottled, translucent. But one was more beautiful than all the others. It was shaped like a butterfly and had a tiny speculum where its head might have been, so faded that reflections barely registered. I bought it on a whim; not for myself, but for Penelope. I thought: it will look so lovely in her hair. Make sure you give it to her at journey's end, Odysseus.'

'You are amazing, Circe,' he replies, as they quit the sty together. 'You do wrong, but I always end up feeling guilty.'

'Lucky bastard,' says Haricot, looking straight at me.

'Lucky?' cries Gumbo, snorting with contempt. 'Luck had nothing to do with it. Pumpkin's time as a pig may be drawing to an end, but he always was and always will be a toad, a fat little toad, a fat little toad forever toadying to the man of the moment, no matter whether it be the Marshal or Odysseus.'

This, I decide, is one insult too many. 'Right now, I'm the man of the moment,' I say. 'So if you want my help to get out of here, you'd better start toadying pronto.'

'Don't push your luck,' says Gumbo. 'The only difference between us is that you believed the whoppers you told were true. That hardly makes you our moral superior.'

'The other difference is that I didn't try to turn Odysseus Junior into a Big Whopper,' I say.

'Why are you two fighting?' demands Chickpea. 'I'm sure that Pumpkin has no intention of abandoning his brothers. After all, we didn't abandon *him* when he lost his marbles in that Sardinian brothel.'

'Sweet Chickpea,' says Gumbo, 'hasn't it occurred to you that our friend's interests are best served by leaving us in this midden? Without us he's got exclusive rights to the story of a lifetime. Our story.'

To which I reply: 'It's obviously slipped your mind that I'm *persona non grata* at the *Dawn*.'

Gumbo's response is immediate and bitter: 'I can think of three vacancies you can try for elsewhere.'

So I say: 'That's in the unlikely event of me getting back to Capsicum in one piece.' Adding: 'At least you'll be safe here, and (what's more) you're going to have a bloody goddess to hump on a regular basis.'

'And what use is that,' replies Gumbo, 'if we can't crow about it to our colleagues?'

I say: 'As I recall, there is some pleasure to be derived from the act itself.'

He says: 'The only act I can contemplate with any

pleasure is this . . .' Then, swinging his head, he hits mine with all his might.

•

When I recover my senses I feel like I am on an operating table under the close scrutiny of a dozen beady eyes. At any rate, numerous faces are looking down at me from a great height. But if they belong to doctors, they are very unusual doctors. None in the profession (so far as I know) sports tusks. Gradually I realize that the heads are not human heads but those of wild boars. Using the remnants of my deductive powers I reach the obvious conclusion: that I am still stymied with my assailant and his cohort. But why are they all so high, and where are the rest of their bodies? And where, for that matter, is mine? I review the length of my torso, and am happy to glimpse ten toes peeping over the pink rotunda of my tummy. Does this mean that Gumbo, Chickpea, and Haricot have been executed for their assault upon me, and their severed crowns placed on my wall as a trophy? Is it my imagination, or is one of them calling my name?

There is no doubt that someone is calling my name, in a voice that is dulcet and (I suddenly realize) very familiar. Nor is it coming from on high. I quickly turn my head to the right and see fair Haidee reclining in an adjacent bed.

'So the corner has been turned,' I say, 'things are getting better.'

Haidee remains silent.

'Aren't they?' I say.

'I don't know, Pumpkin,' she replies. 'The pain is still there. My loss, no less. Circe's greatest cruelty was not to change me into a pig, but to leave my humanity unadulterated. A sow's maternal instinct is not the same as a mother's love. She could have spared me this agony.'

'Time and Telemachus will surely heal it,' I say.

'Poor Telemachus,' she says. 'I overheard what his father said to Circe, and know that he – like any doting parent – would do anything to protect his boy. But how can I hide my secret history from him? To do so would be a form of betrayal. Yet to share it would be to invite rejection. Tell me, Pumpkin, do you still think that things are getting better?'

'Circe got you into this mess, perhaps she can get you out of it,' I say. 'Perhaps among her vast pharmaco-poeia she has a narcotic that aids forgetting?'

'The only drug I'd willingly accept from that woman is hemlock,' replies Haidee.

What is actually offered is an infusion of nepenthe (a herb to soothe the savage breast, says Circe).

'I brought you here (that is, to my hunting lodge),' she says, 'while Odysseus remains in the palace to prepare Telemachus for your reunion. The story is that the pair of you were found wandering half-starved in the forest.'

She places the steaming beakers on the mahogany tables beside our beds. As Circe rises from Haidee's its occupant leaps (naked as she is) for her throat. Circe, caught off guard, falls. Whereupon Haidee straddles her stunned opponent and begins to strangle her.

'This is not because of what you did to me,' she cries, 'but because of what you did to my babies!'

'Not babies but piglets,' gurgles Circe, 'nor did they give their lives in vain.'

Haidee, unmoved by the distinction, continues her dirty work. The sight of her on all fours (not to mention her open arsehole) prompts incapacitating flashbacks, and makes me slow to rise from my bed (anyway, what's the hurry, why shouldn't Circe suffer a little?) Having reluctantly reacquainted myself with the restraints of civilization, I assume the upright position and start to demonstrate the mechanics of bipedalism. Since Haidee remains deaf to my entreaties, I cup the soft underbellies of her breasts, and (with strenuous heaves) separate attacker and victim, thereby saving the former from further sacrilege, and maybe even deicide. She does not thank me (nor, for that matter, does Circe).

'Telemachus has chosen well,' she gasps, gently massaging her neck. 'That girl reminds me of me.

Such a pity his father doesn't have the same good taste.'

Unappeased, Haidee breaks free of my grasp and once again launches herself at the enchantress. This time, however, Circe is on guard. Stepping aside at the last moment like an experienced matador, she grabs Haidee's unbound hair and spins the girl around. Now it's Haidee's windpipe that is vulnerable.

'Mercy,' I cry, 'have mercy!' then block my ears so as to be spared the sound of Haidee's neck snapping. Instead Circe forcibly opens her captive's mouth and pours the entire contents of a beaker down her throat. Once released Haidee tries to regurgitate the liquid, but it soon becomes apparent that it has descended beyond recall.

'Young lady,' says Circe, 'all this violence and disdain for clothes suggests that your animal existence has left a deeper mark than anticipated. Even so I recommend that you put on a dress before you join the others on the boat that awaits.'

'What boat?' says Haidee. 'I'm not going anywhere. I intend to stay on this island, if only to ensure that you suffer exactly as I suffered.'

'That makes perfect sense to me,' says Circe, 'but will it to Telemachus?'

'You are right,' says Haidee, 'how on earth can I explain my anger to him? To tell you the truth, I am beginning to forget its cause myself.'

'We must put our heads together and think of a better reason,' says Circe, 'because I don't want you to go either. If you stay, your husband might be persuaded to place love ahead of duty and stay too, then his old man may just be tempted to do the same (not for love of me, but for love of his son). Like it or not, the spitfire and her prime target have become allies. You may be Odysseus' daughter-in-law, but (as I see it) you are my daughter-in-spirit. As such I hereby appoint you my regent. In my absence (and you know well enough where I'll be) the palace is yours.'

Whatever Haidee swallowed seems to have acted upon her fury like a calming zephyr upon a midsummer storm. Indeed she appears to have entered that trance-like state associated with inner peace. 'My father would be amazed,' she warbles, 'to see his little girl in charge of a palace bigger than his own.'

This time the arm that wraps itself around Haidee's bare shoulder is maternal. 'I am all too familiar with Captain Mandragora and his black deeds,' says Circe, 'but I have heard no word spoken of your real mother. Will you tell me about her?'

'There is nothing to tell,' says Haidee, 'except that she is dead.'

'Of what did she die?' asks Circe.

'Of carelessness,' replies Haidee. 'She mistook toadstools for mushrooms.'

'An unfortunate error, if error it was,' says Circe. 'Do you happen to know what sort they were?'

'I'm not sure,' says Haidee. 'A species that resembled its safer twin; I think my father called them false chanterelles.'

'Ah,' says Circe, 'let me tell you something about the *cortinarius speciosissimus* . . .'

•

The first embrace of Telemachus and Haidee requires the skill of a Renaissance artist to do it justice. First they look into each other's faces while silent tears roll down their cheeks, perhaps to certify that they are not being deceived by an impostor, or a shade dreamed up by false hopes. Then (satisfied) they embrace, as if the one would fall without the support of the other. Not a single word is exchanged. Behind them is an ultra-marine bay and a miniature harbour containing but a single boat, its canvas sail flapping in the wind like a captive bird eager to be free.

'Come,' says Odysseus, enveloping both lovers, 'it is time to board.'

Whereupon Haidee speaks for the first time. 'Forgive me, Telemachus, but I cannot go with you,' she all but whispers. 'I could say with honesty that I have grown too fearful of the sea to risk another voyage, but that would be only half the truth. The other is that I have found a place for myself on Circe's enchanted isle. You are all familiar with my infamous father, of course, but no one (not even you, Telemachus) has enquired after my dear mother. Well, she is dead. She died young and beautiful, having enjoyed a dish of suspect mushrooms. Whether she ate them by accident or by design (because she could no longer coexist with her husband's profession) is not certain. Either way, she died by slow degrees as the poison (only recently identified as orellanin) destroyed her kidneys. Had we but known at the time, she could have been rescued by dialysis and restored to full vigour with a transplant. My father, I have no doubt, would have plucked out one of his own to save her. But we didn't know, and I now believe that it was our ignorance that really killed her. So when Circe informed me about her revolutionary ''pharm'' whose crop is compatible organs, a crop that could have revitalized my poor mother, I felt a duty to volunteer my services. I hardly dare ask this of you, Telemachus, but will you stay here with me?'

I am confounded and confused. Haidee's reason for wishing to stay sounds so plausible and compelling that I am no longer sure whether it (rather than her desire for revenge) is the true motive. But my uncertainty is nothing compared with that of white-faced Telemachus, who has had his happiness restored and threatened within the same moment. He looks help-

lessly toward Odysseus and asks: 'Father, what shall
I do?'

But Odysseus is dumbstruck. He had foreseen every
eventuality but this one: that he would be forced to
complete his journey without his son. He sees (or
supposes he sees) the subtle craft of Circe in action,
her last desperate effort to snare him, but he can think
of no way to counter it. He could point out to Haidee
that her duty to her mother's memory (assuming it is
not a false memory planted by Circe) is no more
important than that Telemachus owes to Penelope, but
it would just make his son's choice that much harder.
So he sets himself a searching question: what would
the boy's mother decide? She would (of course) be
delighted to see Telemachus, but (being honest to a
fault) would also point out that Odysseus had brought
him along less for her sake and more for his own,
because he could not bear to be parted from his son.
And she would be right. No, a good father (if that is
what he is) must not be selfish when his son's happiness is at stake. It will break his heart, but he is
honour-bound to advise his son to stay behind.

'We have been so close for so long,' cries Telemachus, 'and now in a flash we are to be driven apart.
Haidee, you are being too cruel.'

'Telemachus,' she says, 'much as I love you, I cannot
get on that boat.'

'Father,' cries Telemachus, 'is it possible that after today I will never see you again?'

'I will be here always,' says Odysseus, banging his son's chest, 'and parts of me, a nose here, an ear there, will certainly reappear in your children.'

Father and son embrace, while sorrow shakes their bones. Then, turning abruptly, Odysseus strides alone to the quayside.

'It is fitting that I should end my journey without company,' he says wearily, when the rest of us catch up.

At which point Pumpkin unexpectedly takes centre stage.

'Not unless I count for nothing,' I say. 'I have few reasons to remain here, and none to return to Capsicum (a journey that could cost me my life). The only person who would miss me is my beloved mother, and (alas) I am more likely to encounter her in Hades than there. And who knows? I might even meet the Marshal. He died as I was *en route* to interview him. My editor sacked me on account of that misfortune, saying I could only get my job back if I returned with the promised exclusive. I may yet surprise him.'

'Good luck, Pumpkin,' cries everyone, as I take my place beside Odysseus (who, I can tell, thinks me a poor substitute for Telemachus).

'Will you not reconsider and stay also?' whispers Circe, desperately clasping my captain's sleeve.

'When I set out I gave my word that I would not stop until I had discovered Penelope,' he replies. 'It is a pledge I am not prepared to forfeit.'

'Obstinate man!' cries Circe.

'I ask nothing of you,' says Odysseus, 'except that you protect my boy.'

'I will do all in my power,' she replies, 'but as you well know, to have a child is to give a hostage to the fates.'

'Then let us hope that I have suffered enough at their hands for the both of us,' he says, stepping into the boat. I follow his lead.

'Just keep the sails spread wide,' says Circe, 'and the north wind will speed you on your way. Having survived the treacherous river-within-the-sea, you will continue until you reach the most desolate shore of all. Once there it will be necessary to beach this boat. Traverse the land on foot, and you will find the border that separates the living from the dead at a place where two torrential rivers meet: the River of Fire, and the River of Tears. Make your descent and, having reached the bottom, dig a deep trench, which you must fill with libations for the departed (such offerings are already on board). The dead will then appear. Now lift your knife, Odysseus, and sever your ties with land.'

•

For two days our little boat skims across the tops of the waves of its own volition, without even needing a pilot at the helm. On the third we enter an area of dismal mists that completely block out sun and stars. On the fourth the water grows as thick as pitch. On the fifth we reach a deserted cove whose *genius loci* is misery; where whalebacks of grey sand are dotted with blasted stands of black poplars. Abandoning the vessel we approach the nearest copse, only to discover that the branches are heavy with fruit that has withered before its time. The heat from the River of Fire is certainly intense, as is the wailing from the River of Tears.

When we finally stand at the head of the giddy path that (according to Circe) leads directly to Hades, Odysseus says: 'There is no need for you to proceed, Pumpkin. What you have done is already beyond the call of duty. Why not wait here until I return?'

My sentiments entirely, yet I reply: 'Don't forget, I too have my reasons.'

Deep in the earth's dank interior we dig a trench in the mud and fill it with the offerings Circe has provided: milk, honey, and spiced wine, topped off with shiny grains of pearl barley. Odysseus is understandably agitated. After so many hardships his dream is almost within reach. But this knowledge merely increases the tension. Now he has to worry whether the second reunion could possibly meet his expectations.

'Our first was really something,' he says. 'There was shyness and hesitation – how could she be certain that I was really her long-lost husband? – followed by such glorious lovemaking. Believe me, Pumpkin, the intensity of the experience almost justified my wanderings.'

I believe him, all right.

Out of the shadows they emerge, the dead and the buried. Pausing only to lap up the libation, they gather round us greedily as though we had come purposely to see them.

'When you meet my son,' grumbles an old crone, 'be sure to ask him why he never visits his mother.'

Then my own mother spots me and screams: 'What, Pumpkin, is your worthless life at an end so soon?'

'No, Mother,' I say, 'your useless son is by some miracle still numbered among the living.'

'So why are you here then?' she asks.

'To pay my respects where they are due, to accompany my friend . . .' I begin.

'He's still your friend,' exclaims my mother, 'even after you butchered his sweet child?'

'Madam,' says Odysseus, 'excuse my interruption, but you must know that you are doing your son a great injustice. The only thing he did to mine was to save his life.'

'Oh, Pumpkin,' cries my mother, 'can you forgive

me for underestimating you so? I'm afraid that a lifetime in Capsicum has not given me an elevated view
of human nature. Nor has it been improved much by
the company in Hades.'

'Do you count the Marshal among your neighbours?' I ask.

'I have certainly seen the old bastard lording it
among the shades, as if he were still a man of substance,' she replies.

'Excellent,' I say. 'The third reason for my descent
is to beard the Marshal in his new lair, to ask him
those questions I did not know existed until the scales
dropped from my eyes.'

'You see, sir,' says my mother to Odysseus, 'my son
has not lived in vain.'

Nor do I have to wait long to prove my worth. Before
our eyes we see the Marshal lap up our libations like
a thirsty dog. He does not look so good.

'My name is Pumpkin,' I say. 'I was the journalist
you elected to hear your deathbed confession.'

'I remember you,' he replies, 'you're the one everybody called the Court Circular. I must say your
perseverance is admirable.'

'Does that mean you would be prepared to make a
few *post-mortem* observations?' I ask.

'It will be my pleasure,' he replies.

'For the best part of my life I regarded you as
a combination of Odysseus and Achilles,' I say, 'a

mix of wisdom and invincibility.' I look towards my
mother, who is nodding vigorously. 'But now I see you
more as a vampire,' I continue, 'one of the undead
who sucked the life out of the people you ruled. In
short, as someone entirely lacking in humanity.'

'I prefer your first impression, which (as they say)
is often the truer one,' the Marshal replies, 'nor is it
inappropriate. My birth was indeed legend; my mother
was said to be the peasantry, my father the war (which
you are too young to recall). Our enemies asked: "Who
is the Marshal?" Our guns replied: "We are!" Their
strength was my strength. The Federation we established after our great victory wasn't the brainchild of
a cartographer or a diplomat. It was born in blood.
From the outset I knew that only chains could bind
its various peoples together. It is true that I was not so
gentle with those who did not want to be part of the
whole, that I may have upset some nationalists and
intellectuals. But so what? A few novels didn't get
written, a few journalists developed ulcers. Was that
such a big price for all the years of tranquillity? But I
have no need to sing my own praises; the facts are my
propaganda. Just look at what has happened to the
Federation since its great helmsman departed. Are my
successors more humane? Or just weaker? The truth
is that men don't want to be led by their neighbours,
they want to follow legends.'

'But who follows the legend?' I say. 'That's the

problem in a nutshell. You were so suspicious of your colleagues that you failed to groom a successor. The consequence is that the fear and corruption – yes, corruption – you relied upon has crippled the body politic. While you lived, your strength was sufficient to suppress the symptoms, but in your absence the disease has emerged full-blown.'

'You are right,' replies the Marshal, 'there is a sickness, a stink of dead fish. But your diagnosis is hopelessly naive; mild paranoia and fiscal malfeasance are no more dangerous than the common cold. It requires something a lot worse to finish off a human being, let alone a nation. Something like what did me in: a nasty combination of prostate cancer and angina. Immediately after an operation for the former I began pissing buckets of blood, apparently a side effect of the tablets I was taking to combat the latter. My doctors put their heads together and decided that I could not afford to lose so much blood. So they embargoed my cardiovascular pills. The bleeding stopped all right, but I was blessed with daily bouts of angina pectoris instead. Tough luck! I could live with a little heartache (though not with the fucking heart attack they failed to anticipate). My biggest regret on first arriving in Hades was that I did not survive long enough to execute those incompetent quacks, but now (thanks to you, Pumpkin), I see that they were entirely justified. If I could return today I would be writing exactly the same prescription for my people. I would present them with the same choice I faced: would they rather live with a little heartache (a little less than their hearts' desire), or would they prefer to bleed to death? You call me a bloodsucker. Doesn't that prove that I'm anything but?'

'I apologize for likening you to Count Dracula,' I say. 'On second thoughts you're more like a stern father-figure who has outlived his function. You always treated your people like children; as a consequence many of us now find it impossible to act as responsible adults.'

'Wrong again, Pumpkin,' replies the Marshal. 'The Anchovies didn't take up arms against the Federation on account of bad potty-training, but because they are once again in thrall to my old enemy, the dictatorship of the heart. That is what has always been wrong with the world. Too many people privilege the heart, not enough the head. Perhaps you are right, Pumpkin, perhaps I was a wicked old tyrant, but I recognized that essential truth. Your friend Odysseus (who is just about to attain his heart's desire) will soon back me up, of that I have no doubt.'

But Odysseus is no longer listening. He has singled out a woman among the multitude of shadows.

'Pumpkin,' he shouts, 'meet the wife!'

'Odysseus,' cries the woman, 'is it really you? Have

you remained loyal even though I eloped with the one suitor no woman can resist?'

'Nor any man defeat,' adds Odysseus.

'How is our son?' she asks. 'How is dear Telemachus?'

'Happiness stopped him in his tracks,' replies Odysseus, 'he has a wife.'

'And children?' asks Penelope eagerly.

'Not yet,' replies Odysseus, 'but when their first daughter comes she will be named Penelope.'

'You have not changed, husband,' says the original Penelope.

'Nor you,' replies Odysseus. 'In fact I have a present to complement your beauty,' he adds, handing her Circe's tortoiseshell comb.

'What a gorgeous thing,' she says, carefully placing it in her dark hair, where its tiny mirror reflects the available light.

Unable to restrain himself any longer, Odysseus lunges at the tantalizing moonstone that crowns his lovely wife. Three times, with ever-growing desperation, he tries to clasp Penelope; three times she proves as insubstantial as the smoke from her pyre, leaving only the tortoiseshell comb in his hands. My mind returns to the beach at Endive, and to the little dog that chased reflections in the sand.

'Sweet wife,' he begs, 'how I long to hold you. Why

can't we be granted some comfort by feeling one another's flesh?'

'Have you forgotten, Odysseus, that I am no longer flesh and bone, but only ash?' cries Penelope. 'What you see is but a wraith.'

'Then am I to have no reward for all my travails?' wails Odysseus.

'Is the knowledge that I am still your loyal wife not enough?' asks Penelope sadly.

'Forgive my outburst,' says Odysseus. 'To witness memories made flesh was more than I could stand.'

'And that is why you must live out your remaining days in the world of substance and light,' says Penelope. 'Farewell, my once and future husband. Don't forget to tell our son what you have seen.' With that she is gone, one more dim shadow in a never-ending procession.

•

We are standing by the boat on the grey beach. 'Where shall we go?' I ask Odysseus. 'I don't know, Pumpkin,' he says. 'Perhaps back to Circe's island, if only to see my son again. Knowing my luck it may take a while. Are you with me?'

'I just need to take a pee,' I say, wondering whether my internal commissar will permit me to water the dead poplars, but knowing that the uncertainty is precisely what makes Pumpkin Pumpkin.

The Naked and the Dead

For love is strong as death;
jealousy is cruel as the grave . . .

The Song of Songs

i

The blizzard is a novelty verging on the miraculous. No one alive has seen snow fall upon San Francisco. Opening the window of my apartment I expose my face to the elements and receive an icy kiss upon the lips, a kiss that awakens me from my melancholy torpor.

All afternoon I monitor the hissing flakes as they dance around the street lamps like albino moths. The city, with its roller-coaster roads, has been rendered impassable, but what is that to me? My father's prophecy has come true.

A long time ago, when I was but a whining schoolboy on the cusp of puberty, one of my teachers (an idle, careless man) had ordered the class to compose a story that had to conclude with the line: 'Nothing remains but the tracks in the snow.' All my fellow pupils proceeded to recycle half-remembered yarns about doomed expeditions to the South Pole, or

batty excursions to the Himalayas in pursuit of the
Yeti. I was no exception, until my mind wandered to
the nubile beauties in our midst. Inspired by their
bodies I immediately eschewed the dime-novel muse
and penned a romance set in our own neighbourhood.
I wrote of what I knew (or thought I knew). My story
spoke of the agonies of teenage desire, of the curse of
unspoken love. It did not end tragically, but it did not
end happily either; the star-crossed pair parted for the
last time on a night such as this, when she flounced
off in a yellow cab, and he remained on the street
corner, with nothing to do but contemplate the tread-
marks in the virgin snow. I thought I had done well.
'Originality is praiseworthy,' announced my Reality
Instructor, as he delivered my first rejection slip, 'but
even originality can be overdone. Elephants do not
roam the streets of Manhattan, and it never snows in
San Francisco. Any story that depends upon such an
outlandish phenomenon is doomed to be a dud.'
Even after so many years I want to rub the pompous
swine's nose in the stuff steadily accumulating in
the street below. Like the non-existent pachyderms of
Manhattan, I do not forget.

I remember returning from school crestfallen, and
confessing the cause to my parents. My mother cursed
the pedagogue and all his progeny to the nth generation. My father offered a more considered response.
'We are distantly related to the meshuga Jew who

called himself Emperor Norton and fancied that he ruled San Francisco,' he said. 'His subjects, being an indulgent bunch, humoured him, and he went to his grave (accompanied by ten thousand mourners) with his delusion of grandeur intact. Perhaps it wasn't a delusion. If everyone subscribes to the same delusion, who's to say it's not true? Before he died the ersatz Emperor decreed that a bridge should be built across the Golden Gate, where the mighty Pacific rushes into the Bay, a task deemed to be beyond human ingenuity. Until an engineer named Joseph Strauss (another Jew, I may add) came up with a solution so elegant I still weep when I think of it. Know-it-alls like your teacher pointed to the treacherous waters and called him a second Emperor Norton. You only have to look out of the window to see how wrong they were. In all probability you will one day see something equally unlikely, something like snow falling on the city.'

That homily was typical. It is no exaggeration to state that my father idolized Joseph Strauss. He regarded his masterpiece as a paradigm, a manifestation of his own essential optimism, an ever-present confirmation of his belief that what seems impossible today will eventually come to pass somewhere, if not tomorrow, then a century hence. The Museum of the City of San Francisco holds a series of pictorial folders, commissioned by the Associated Oil Company, that record every stage of the bridge's construction. Each folio (of which there are six) consists of one 8×10 photograph accompanied by explanatory text. 'The photographers,' the museum notes, 'are not identified.' Well, I can name one: my father.

Of all the assignments he undertook in his long career as a commercial photographer none gave him greater satisfaction. Not because he considered the photographs as being in any way artistic or distinguished, but simply because he felt himself uniquely privileged to have been able to witness the creation of a latter-day wonder, a modern rival to the Colossus of Rhodes. At any rate, he always displayed that portfolio with particular pride. It might seem perverse, but the image that really astounded me was not one that featured the marvellous structure's constituent parts – its massive anchorages and soaring towers, its sweeping cables and endless deck – but one that was marked by its total absence; a panorama of the straits before they were bridged. To tell the truth, it delivered a real shock, being a reminder that even world-famous landmarks are transient, with a before and – by implication – an after. I felt the same unease whenever I saw a photograph of my parents taken prior to my entry into the world, demonstrating the unwelcome news that they (and it) could exist very well without me.

Actually there was one other photograph that sent shivers down my spine. My father took it from the top of the Marin Tower. All 746 feet of it. How he managed it is beyond me. Merely looking at the cables beetling down like a ski slope on a glass mountain made me feel dizzy. Unlike the fellow running up one of them, as boldly as Blondin at Niagara. Whenever my mother saw the photograph she always wept and said the same thing: 'My brother had a head for heights like he was a Mohawk Indian, much good it did him.'

Despite the best efforts of nay-sayers and monopoly capitalists, construction finally began in 1933 (a black year for European Jewry). In America the Great Depression was at its worst and thousands flocked to the site seeking jobs, among them my fearless uncle. They were in luck. Joseph Strauss was not my father's hero for nothing. He was a good boss. The best. Insisting upon the most rigorous safety precautions in the history of bridge building. Hard hats were worn for the first time, not to mention glare-free goggles. A cream was even formulated by cosmeticians to protect exposed skin from the hostile elements. However, the most conspicuous prophylactic of all was a vast safety net suspended beneath the deck from end to end. 'People used to show up with car-loads of kids,' recalled my father, 'as if they thought that the construction site was merely a feint of hand, stagecraft, a circus.' Occasionally the kiddies received a jolt that informed them otherwise. Nineteen men fell at one time or another, and would have perished but for the net. They called themselves the Half-Way-To-Hell Club. In those days the norm was one man killed for every million dollars spent. The Golden Gate Bridge cost thirty-five million dollars, and in four years had claimed but a single life.

And then, only three months shy of completion, a section of scaffolding broke free and plummeted into the safety net, taking a dozen poor souls with it. For a few moments it looked as if the rigging would hold and the workers would be spared, as the others had been. But no, it was but a temporary stay of execution. Neptune's trident ripped the invincible net apart, dropping the unlucky men into the maelstrom below. Even then two were saved. But ten drowned, one of whom was my uncle. They fished him from his watery grave and buried him properly in the Hills of Eternity Memorial Park. Joseph Strauss paid for the funeral, of course. 'I often relive his last moments in the safety net,' whispered my mother to the stranger beside her, 'and I do my best to save him. I try to force the hairs on his arm to thicken into filaments that will in turn produce barbs. I try to make his newly feathered wings spread and flap, so that the uplift will carry him free. But I always fail, and he drops like a stone.' The stranger wrapped a consoling arm around the unknown woman's shoulder. They were married as soon as the year of mourning was at an end, and in the fullness of time named their first-born after the dead man.

The Golden Gate Bridge opened on 27 May 1937. Thousands turned out, as if a collective decision had been taken to applaud this great feat of levitation, and to sustain it with the willing suspension of their disbelief. How else would travellers be able to cross the terrifying void in safety? The trailblazer was a cowboy on a palomino. I like to think my father had a hand in that. He came from the east, but he was crazy about Westerns. He admired Gary Cooper, Joel McCrea, Henry Fonda, James Stewart, Randolph Scott *et alii*, but his true love was John Wayne. He never missed one of his hero's movies. Nor did his son. John Ford was our favourite director, but when it came to Westerns we were catholics. I was about ten when my father took me to see Alan Ladd in *Shane*. Of course I had already witnessed baddies bite the dust a million times (not to mention the odd unfortunate goodie), but that movie contained my first actual interment. I watched with growing alarm as the pall-bearers lowered Stonewall's pine coffin into a rectangular hole, and felt for the first time the full force of the tragedy that had befallen my namesake. I grasped the literal meaning of the word 'deceased', and understood that one day I too would fall through the safety net and into the insatiable earth. The more I thought

of the hereafter, the more I liked the now. And the
here.

•

I begged to be allowed to explore our neighbourhood
on my own, much to the consternation of my parents.
'As Joseph Strauss was to his workers, so would we
be to you,' explained my father. 'Ever-vigilant guardians. It is restricting, that is true, but it is always for
your own good. Nevertheless, you wish to exercise
your right to discover the world for yourself, to be your
own Christopher Columbus. We applaud your spirit
of adventure. But we also remember that all Joseph
Strauss's precautions couldn't save your uncle from
the evil eye. This is why we are so reluctant to let you
go, even though we acknowledge that we must.'

One day I ventured further than I had ever done
before, hiked the full length of undiscovered roads,
and found myself on a haunted headland. Site of the
old Sutro Baths. Deserted now, they had, in their
heyday, attracted thousands with their endless novel-
ties. People paid five cents to travel out on the new
railroad so that they could gawk at freaks of nature,
at manatees, hermaphrodites, and mermaids, at beasts
with human voices; so that they could wonder at the
marvels of the ancient world; and, above all, so that
they could relax in the salty pools of the baths themselves. Contemporary prints, still pinned to the walls

of neighbourhood restaurants, confirmed the area's former glory: showed city folk in their Sunday best gazing in awe at a Kubla Khanish confection made of iron and glass. The baths relied upon the tides, and the ebb and flow of fashion. Unfortunately the latter ebbed but failed to flow. Indifference and a fire of unexplained origins destroyed the crystal palace, until nothing remained but a row of empty tanks that endlessly echoed the sneezing ocean.

On the cliffs above the ruins stood a box-like building fashioned to resemble a camera. A periscope protruded from its roof. 'Welcome, young man, welcome to the city's finest camera obscura,' said its proprietor, who looked as if he had just swum across from Seal Rock. His hair was jet black, as was his thick moustache, not to mention his shiny oilskin. A frisky pup snapped at his heels. 'Leonardo da Vinci, no less, built one of the first. In his backyard, would you believe? Scared the living daylights out of his neighbours. Know what they thought?' He chuckled at the superstitions of the Florentines. 'That the *genius loci* had sold his soul to the devil in exchange for a mirror that showed both past and future. Can't promise you that, my lad, but you will surely see the present in all its glory.'

I handed over the entrance fee and entered the giant camera. 'The periscope only takes six minutes to complete its circuit,' explained my guide, 'but a bright spark like you can linger as long as you please. Why, only last week someone stayed for seven whole hours. Who knows what he saw? Not just the outside world, I'll be bound, but an inner landscape too. I've seen many a grown man moved to tears on account of it. And I'm talking about the sort of man who hasn't cried since his first dog died. Pluto!' he yelled, addressing his own sandy-haired hound. 'Leave the child alone. Don't worry,' he said, turning to me, 'he wouldn't hurt a fly. Between you and me, he's a bit simple-minded. That's why I call him Pluto. After the Walt Disney character, not the god of the infernal regions. You can pet him if you like.' So saying, he patted me on the shoulder, and departed.

In the centre of the sombre room was a parabolic dish. What did I expect to see projected upon its concavity? The history of the patch re-enacted by ghosts? Ohlone Indians on their haunches scoffing abalone? The *Golden Hind* dropping anchor? Zorro carving up cruel Capitan Monastario as if he were the Sunday roast? Long-dead day trippers enjoying the revitalizing air? In fact the images the rotating periscope captured were more quotidian but no less eerie. As my eyes adjusted to the gloom I saw that the bowl was filled with nothing but the silent waves of the vacant ocean. I thought immediately of the Bible's first word (recently drummed into me at cheder): *B'reshit*: 'In the beginning . . . darkness was on the face of the deep.' But the all-seeing eye was not static, and the image changed as the lens turned.

Gradually, rocks emerged from the ocean, populated by slimy creatures from its depths; gulls and cormorants congregated in the heavens above. Next, the mainland was formed. Men and women frolicked on its strand; dogs chased their tails. The lens moved on. Civilization flourished. Cars filled parking lots. High-rise apartments stretched to the horizon. Then suddenly it was all gone; the land and all that was on it. Nothing remained but the enigmatic waves rolling across the surface of the ocean. I had witnessed the history of the world, from creation to apocalyptic flood, compressed into six minutes. All for a quarter.

Ten times I watched the world begin and end, until I became obsessed with preserving the images that flourished so briefly. Knowing that I could never hold them all within my fallible memory, I decided there and then to be a photographer like my father, to dedicate my life to fixing those fleeting moments.

My father continued to photograph the Golden Gate Bridge until the end of his days, as if to provide continuing evidence that it was real, and not some collective hallucination. One of his last studies shows it apparently resting upon a foundation of fog. Although the image is particularly beautiful, the phenomenon is hardly uncommon. Unlike present conditions, which I am honour-bound to experience.

It is both a family responsibility and a civic duty to record the bridge dressed with snow. I load my Olympus with Tri-X. Braving the arctic blitzkrieg I hit Lombard Street and begin to walk down the hill towards Stockton. Except that walking is impossible. So I place the camera around my neck and toboggan to the intersection on my backside. As it turns out, every junction is marked by the meeting of a vehicle in unstoppable descent with an unfortunate representative of cross-traffic. Of the passengers there is no trace except (*nota bene*, you old bastard) the tracks in the snow. Crashes of every description and a few tumbles of my own punctuate the erratic procession to Fisherman's Wharf. The waterfront is deserted and dark; there are no sounds save the howling of the wind, the motion of the ocean, and the barking of seals. To the south, automobiles are moving slowly and silently along the Bay Bridge beneath a diffused canopy of light. Continuing through Crissy Field I mistake the chiming of frozen eucalyptus leaves for the Snow Queen's sleigh bells, and wonder who now would rescue me from her Ice Palace. Branches, unprepared for the extra burden, snap. Whole trees creak and tumble to the ground with a heart-rending sigh. My extremities, equally unacclimatized, are the sport of biting cold. And then, at last, my reward, the icing on the cake: thick snow upon the Golden Gate Bridge.

Blowing hard to revive my hands, I shoot a roll to honour my late father, and another for posterity.

It is common knowledge that suspension bridges depend upon gravity for their essential stability. I also utilized gravity in order to reach my destination. But gravity becomes my enemy when I try to make the final ascent to my apartment on Lombard and Grant. After several failed attempts I am forced to take shelter inside *Tobaccus*, a bar built to resemble a smouldering filter tip (that is to say, an ochre drum topped off with a ring of red neon), where a few other refugees are cradling steaming thimbles of espresso or shots of fiery grappa. Despite the weather the waitresses are all wearing togas, cut in the classical style to reveal cleavage and thigh. Awaiting my first ice-breaker I register the arrival of a new customer. Noticing me, she waves frantically, as though she were my date. In fact our meeting is a coincidence, though I know her well enough: Angelika Ikon, picture editor at a magazine called *Pays Inconnu* (also known as Pays My Bills).

'I was under the impression that the Sierras and the Pacific were supposed to protect us from such things,' she says, shaking the snow from her hair. 'I can only think that someone hereabouts has offended Boreas big-time.' Pulling out a chair she says: 'I'll join you if I may.'

Referring to the camera around her neck, I ask: 'Get any good shots?'

'The Bay Bridge looked spectacular,' she replies, 'and Union Square was interesting. Otherwise nothing much. It's very hard to get around.'

'I know,' I say. 'I can't even make it home.'

'That's handy,' says Angelika Ikon, 'because I have a bone to pick with you. I don't know who upset the god of the north wind, but I do know who's got right up my nose. I'm looking straight at him.'

So she tells me how she has just been reading a terrible story on the front page of the *Chronicle*, all about the violation and butchering of a young woman on Mount Tamalpais. The story continued on one of the inside pages, right opposite a letter from yours truly defending the work of Les Krims. It needed defending because a few days previously a notorious harpie had openly defaced a set of his tasteless photographs housed in the library of a nearby university. I found her action objectionable, and said so in my communication. Unfortunately the newspaper had chosen to augment my argument with a reproduction of one of the offending images, which could equally have illustrated the story that had caught Angelika Ikon's eye.

A brunette was stretched full-length on a cold kitchen floor; supine, naked (of course), arms bound behind her back. Dark liquid apparently flowed from her derrière. There were more o'er-spilling wounds on her belly, chest, and arms. The victim (rather,

sacrifice) faced the viewer, her sightless eyes need-
lessly occluded by shades. A handkerchief had been
stuffed into her mouth. She was dark-haired, fore and
aft. A Coca-Cola bottle stood upright within the triangle formed by her folded left leg and outstretched
right (the longest and loveliest leg you ever saw). Who
did this to her? Dumped her, plucked and trussed, in
her own kitchen, oven-ready, at the foot of her own
oven (like the unfortunate heroine of a bleak fairy
tale)? She was staring blankly at the only clue, the
beast's trademark, a pile of pancakes, a feature of all
the photographs in the set. Hence its collective title,
'The Incredible Case of the Stack o'Wheats Murders'.

'I was less than convinced by your effort to decrimi-
nalize Les Krims,' continues Angelika Ikon. 'And when
I read that you were turned on by images of voluptuous
nudes lying in puddles of blood, I have to tell you
that I was very tempted to terminate our working
relationship.'

'For one thing, it wasn't blood but chocolate syrup,'
I reply. 'As you well know, the photos were parodies.
They were meant to be amusing. For another, they
were extremely erotic. What purpose would it have
served to pretend otherwise? Would you have thought
more of me if I had lied, if I had counterfeited distaste?'

Her hiss of contempt would have impressed a boa
constrictor. 'You flatter yourself that you are being
honest,' she scoffs, 'but your so-called "frankness" is

nothing but a self-serving sham, a sham contrived to shield you from your own culpability. It is true that you didn't actually wield the knife on Mount Tamalpais. But the hand that did was the agent of your unspoken desires. Like it or not, you were the killer's accomplice.'

'Bullshit!' I cry, striking the table so forcefully that my grappa wobbles and spills. 'Do you think I didn't recognize horror as well as sexuality in the disposition of the models?'

'They don't need your pity,' she snaps.

'Of course they don't,' I protest, 'they aren't really dead.'

'Would it have made any difference if they were?' asks Angelika Ikon. 'What if the chocolate syrup really was what it appeared to be? What if the women really had been stabbed? Would you still have got a hard-on?'

'Another grappa?' the toga-toting waitress with the deep-pan cleavage enquires grumpily of me. Questions! Questions! I reply in the affirmative to the latter. As to the former, I hold my fire, although I am all too aware of the honest response to the challenge.

'What's the matter?' sneers my companion. 'Have I touched on a truth that dare not speak its name? I must say, I admire your wife's courage. How many years have you been married? Ten? Fifteen? I don't think I'd feel safe sleeping under the same roof as you for even

one night.' And then, as if she has suddenly remembered her manners, she asks: 'How is she, by the way?
I was sorry to learn of her new misfortune.'

'She's coping,' I say, 'but at the same time there's
no denying the fact that she's a changed woman. Not
that the experience hasn't changed me too.'

'Now you come to mention it,' says Angelika Ikon,
'there is something different about you. I can see it in
your eyes. They seem dimmer. As though a light had
been extinguished within. Of course I wouldn't know
about your wife, never having had the pleasure.
Indeed, I've sometimes asked myself if she actually
exists, and isn't just a figment of your overactive
imagination.'

I assure Angelika Ikon that she does, and lest you
have any doubts yourselves, let me show you a photograph or two to prove it. Here's one, taken just before
we swore to forsake all others. She is under the
blankets of a promiscuous bed. Supine but awake,
definitely awake. Her eyes are open, open but glazed.
The indifferent covers do not hide her nakedness. A
pale breast is exposed, like some nocturnal creature
caught by the wheaty light of early morning. The same
western sun illuminates forehead and hair. Her lips –
still in the nightshade – have grown plump from too
many kisses. How lovely she was, how lovely.

I met her for the first time at a rerun of *The
Searchers*. Neither of us was yet twenty. We had

adjoining seats and were both unaccompanied, though we only became acquainted as a result of a post-screening accident. Shuffling along the row towards the aisle I clumsily stepped on her foot.

'Sorry,' I said.

'Never apologize,' she replied, 'it's a sign of weakness.'

'John Wayne?' I said, acknowledging the reference.

'Who else?' she replied.

We discussed his role in the movie we had just seen over coffee and strudel in a local café. Only then did we exchange names.

'Don't be fooled by mine,' said my future wife. 'It would have you believe that I am of Sephardic descent, that my soul yearns for Toledo, and my ear for Ladino. But so-called Alma Perera had no affinity for Spanish at school. Nor was her complexion olive. In short, I have long suspected that I am not her, but someone else entirely; someone with an interesting tale to tell, if only I could remember it. Which is why I often recall something I once heard John Wayne say.'

'In what movie?' I asked, considering myself an aficionado.

'It wasn't in a movie,' she said, 'it was in his garden.'

It took a moment to register. 'You knew John Wayne?' I gasped.

'Why not?' she replied. 'I lived in Hollywood till I was twelve, and was educated at Gomorrah Professional High, along with his kids. It was not like other schools; where else do lessons end at lunchtime, so that the pupils can pursue their movie careers in the afternoon? Those of us who weren't child stars hung around each other's houses. On my first visit to the Duke's I was introduced as German. Don't ask me why. He was very sweet and insisted upon addressing me in my mother tongue (which I actually knew better than Spanish). *"Kennen wir uns nicht?"* he said as we shook hands. *Don't we know each other?* Later I overheard him say to one of his cronies (in English): "Her eyes, her lips, her voice, her hair, even her figure, they all remind me of someone; damned if I can remember who." One day I'm going to trace that missing person; the real me.'

When I told my parents about this fateful encounter, my father immediately exclaimed: 'With John Wayne as matchmaker you've got no choice. Marry the girl!' Fittingly enough I first glimpsed her naked breasts through the viewfinder of the Yashica he had presented to me on the occasion of my bar mitzvah. At the time my future wife was sitting on the edge of her parent's double bed wearing nothing but a hundred-dollar brassiere and silk knickers. 'Why not slip off the top half?' I suggested. She shrugged, then obliged. As I pressed the shutter a black cat emerged from behind her back and tiptoed across the immaculate sheet. Ere long I was given license to roam all over my intended's body. Even so, her response to posing remained the same: 'I have no problem with breasts, but my private parts must remain precisely that.' It took a small earthquake to change her mind.

Looking at these early photographs, a perceptive observer (such as yourself) might note the excessive number of hundred-dollar bras that tend to peep from under various beds like pairs of baggy-eyed spectacles. The reason is that my future wife, frugal to the point of asceticism in every other respect, had a weakness for expensive underwear. She blamed her mother, a devotee of haute couture, who had introduced her only child to a bespoke manufacturer as soon as her breasts were sufficiently mature. Mother and daughter had taken an elevator to the third floor of a neoclassical emporium on Maiden Lane and rung the bell beside a heavy door (discreetly unmarked). They were welcomed as if they had come to take tea. Indeed my late mother-in-law was served fragrant darjeeling in a transparent cup. Meanwhile my destined bride was ushered to a cubicle, where she was required to disrobe. Eventually she was visited by a severe woman in a white coat who wore her hair in a bun. The barebreasted girl (my wife-in-waiting) fully expected to see a stethoscope draped around the creature's neck. In fact there was nothing more sinister than a tape measure, which was immediately put to good use. The figures were recorded obsessively in a thick notebook bound with alligator hide. The new client was tickled by the old hand's intensity, and was unable to prevent her amusement from showing.

'Why are you smiling, child?' asked the woman.

'You take your work so seriously,' said the innocent (who would one day be my wife).

'On your wedding day you may thank me,' replied the woman sternly, 'but on your twenty-fifth anniversary you will certainly bless me. Now lean forwards and gently pour yourself into the cups. Don't look so dubious, my pretty miss. A properly fitted brassiere is an absolute necessity if you want your breasts to retain their youthful perfection.' Her new husband certainly had no complaints.

Our honeymoon got off to a bad start. We sideswiped the deer around midnight, at an anonymous location somewhere between our starting point and our hideaway. It leapt out from the obscurity straight into our path. The Impala struck it broadsides. I heard a thump as metal pounded flesh and the sound of breaking glass as the right headlamp shattered. I saw the broken creature framed briefly in my rear-view mirror as it somersaulted across the blacktop into eternity. 'Don't stop,' cried my wife, 'whatever you do don't stop! I couldn't bear it.' It felt like sacrilege, but I humoured her, and continued one-eyed and dented until I saw a sign that said: 'Vacancy.'

The reception was still illuminated, and there was a fat woman within watching television.

'I live in hope of catching a rerun of "You Bet Your Life",' she said, 'to remind myself of the unlikely fact that I was once one of its resident glamour-girls. Mr Marx was a funny man, you know, but very rude. Pinched my backside at every opportunity. Take my word for it: in those days it was worth pinching.' She looked out of the window at the car. 'Your wife not feeling well?' she asked.

'A bit upset,' I conceded.

'You're newly-weds,' she said, 'or my name ain't Golda.' She threw me the key. 'Now go and make up to her. And don't spare the sheets.'

'If the gods have a bone to pick, it's with me, not you,' said my wife. 'You couldn't help hitting it, but I chose not to stop.'

•

When my parents died I inherited the apartment on Lombard and Grant in which I had grown to manhood. By that time I was a wildlife photographer with a local reputation. I was drawn irresistibly to the ocean: to the evil-smelling elephant seals at Año Nuevo, to the barnacled grey whales at Davenport, to the beach-bound fossils at Capitola, to the cypresses and chest-thumping sea otters at Point Lobos. Not to mention the birds, from honey-dipping hummers to

kamikaze pelicans. And the trees. Most of the work
was commissioned by Angelika Ikon and appeared
subsequently in *Pays Inconnu*. Meanwhile my
wife, a disciple of Bruno Bettelheim, had developed
a demanding career redeeming crazy adolescents.
Another eternal optimist (like my father), she excelled
at pacifying the agitated mind, at turning the snarling
lycanthrope into teacher's pet. She knew that love was
not enough; so she gave them love, and planned to
offer them more. Her ambition was to become a child
psychologist, which required her to undergo a period
of self-analysis.

At first she changed shrinks like others changed
shoes; tried Freudians, Jungians, Kleinians, Adlerians,
and even a Reichian. But the one that fitted the best
was a Mesmerist, a magus who practised hypno-
therapy.

After just one session my wife breathlessly
announced that a breakthrough was on the way. 'Some
amazing stuff is coming out,' she revealed.

Shortly thereafter the genius coined a neologism for
her condition: inherited amnesia. 'Not an unreasonable diagnosis,' said my wife, 'given that my mother's
mother really was an orphan.'

After the following session she said: 'I'd be obliged
if you would accompany me to my next appointment.
You have to witness what's happening for yourself.
Otherwise you'll have me certified.'

'Won't I be trespassing?' I asked.

'My shrink doesn't mind,' she replied. 'As for me . . .
I have no secrets from you.'

'What's it like,' I said, 'being hypnotized?'

'Strange,' she replied, 'but not unpleasant. At first
it's like being dazzled by an oncoming car. Your eyes
fill with tears and the world becomes blurred and
indistinct. Then your thoughts turn disorderly, as they
do on the edge of sleep. But you do not fall asleep,
though you are certainly not awake either. You see
things as if in an enormous bowl, shadowy figures
that live for but a few moments.'

For legal reasons I am unable to call Doctor X by
his proper name. His consulting rooms, whither we
went, were on the higher reaches of Twin Peaks. Vene-
tian blinds made the interior resemble the set of a
black and white movie.

'Any relative of this wonderful lady is a friend of
this practice,' he said, with all the sincerity of a Greek
bearing gifts. 'Tell me,' he whispered conspiratorially,
'has she shared any of our marvellous discoveries with
you?'

'I think she's been holding fire on that,' I replied.

'Perhaps she wanted to surprise you,' he said. 'But
before you witness the practice, let me fill you in on
the theory. When Aeneas went to visit his old man
in the Underworld he was permitted to see certain
souls, penned deep in a green vale, that were destined

for recycling. It is my opinion that we all give house room to old souls. It is simply that most of us live in unhappy ignorance of the fact. Your wife is a rare exception. It's not by accident that her name means ''soul'' in Spanish.'

She was sitting in an armchair staring fixedly at a faceted piece of glass which Doctor X held a few inches above her forehead. It looked slightly grotesque, like the eye of a fly with a serious thyroid problem.

'See how the concentration forces her pupils to contract,' Doctor X whispered. 'This stage does not last long. Soon she will be completely relaxed.'

To prove his point he made several passes over my wife's face with his free hand, without provoking any response. Not even a blink.

'Now look carefully at her eyes,' he said. 'See how the pupils have already dilated.'

It was true: the pupils had all but eclipsed the irises. Moreover, the eyeballs themselves appeared to be protruding.

'You may also observe,' added the shrink, 'that your wife's respiration has slackened considerably. This is often accompanied by an increased flow of saliva.' Sure enough, my wife was dribbling.

Having dispensed with the glass bauble, Doctor X closed my wife's unresisting lids with the tips of his fingers and gently stroked her cheeks. As he did so her eyelids began to vibrate rapidly, as they always do when a sleeper dreams vividly. 'I think we are ready to begin,' he said.

'Can you hear me?' the shrink asked.

My wife nodded slowly.

'Would you mind introducing yourself?' he continued.

'Don't be silly, Doc,' she replied, 'you know me well enough. I'm Wyatt's girl.'

'And what does your old boyfriend think of this new dalliance?' the hypnotist enquired.

'My former fiancé, Mr Johnny Behan, who made no objections to me becoming a whore, cannot abide me being courted by another man,' said my wife. 'To tell you the truth, Doc, he and Mr Earp have become terrible enemies. So much so that every time I hear a shot – and there are an abundance of them in Tombstone – I picture my dear Wyatt falling before the gunfire of that green-eyed monster or one of his horrible cronies.'

'I think I can hear shooting now,' said the shrink urgently. 'As many as twenty or thirty rounds.'

My wife screamed. I moved towards her, but Doctor X laid a restraining hand upon my shoulder.

'The moment I have always dreaded has arrived,' she sighed dreamily. 'Someone has tried to murder my darling. Wyatt always warned me to keep out of the way if trouble ever started. But how can I stay safely indoors when my lover's lifeblood might be leaking into the dust? There's no time to dress properly, no time to put on a bonnet. I am running into the street, waving my arms like a madwoman. The first wagon ignores me, but the second stops. It carries me to the corner of Fourth and Fremont, near the OK Corral, where I am confronted by a bloody tableau of the quick and the dead. Billy Clanton has gone to his maker, as have the two McLaury boys. I watch aghast as Morgan and Virgil, Wyatt's brothers, are stretchered from the scene. But where is my beloved? Where is Wyatt himself? I all but swoon when I spot him upright and very much alive. I jump from the wagon and start to run across the street, all the while saying a little prayer: "Dear God, I haven't got a bonnet on. If Wyatt notices please don't let him think badly of me." '

'I hope you don't think badly of me,' said my wife *in propria persona* as we returned to Lombard and Grant.

'Of course not,' I said. 'I just think you've been watching too many Westerns.' Surely my wife – an otherwise rational creature – hadn't fallen for this mumbo-jumbo, this witch-doctory? To judge by her loyalty to Dr X she certainly had. Anyway, I lost interest in such speculations when she unexpectedly gave me reason to think very badly of her indeed.

•

Every August I spend a few days photographing leopard sharks and bat rays from a kayak at Moss Landing, but a couple of years ago a burnt-out clutch in our ageing Impala confined me to the city. Listening idly to the radio I heard that an out-of-sync grey whale had come to grief at Land's End; having nothing better to do I gathered my equipment and took a bus to the end of Geary. However, my intention was immediately forgotten when I noticed, to my astonishment, that the camera obscura was still in operation. And there was faithful Pluto, now distinctly grey around the chops. In the intervening years his owner had come to resemble an ancient walrus with his white whiskers and off-white suit. He beckoned me over.

'There used to be at least three camera obscuras in the city,' he barked, by way of greeting. 'Not any more. This fella is the last of the Mohicans.' He tapped the wall affectionately with his cane. 'Believe me, sir, it's an experience not to be missed. Like dropping acid, only a mite cheaper. How to describe its effect?' He shrugged. 'All I can say is that time operates differently in there, as does the optic nerve. Best see for yourself. What have you got to lose? I do not believe there is another place hereabouts that offers enlightenment for just a dollar.'

As I once again watched the dish rotate with its ever-changing cargo, I felt like an Olympian deity and began to plot all kinds of futures for the anonymous and unsuspecting pedestrians. Until someone known to me by name appeared unexpectedly.

At least, someone closely resembling my wife was strolling along the windswept esplanade with an unknown colleague. I watched the couple – who seemed deep in animated conversation – until they vanished. As if they had never existed. I did not weep, but felt strangely bereaved, like the widow of some pre-Columbian navigator. I ran outside, but found no comfort there; no familiar face, only the indifferent stares of strangers. This dismal premonition remained a palpable burden, and so it was a great relief when my wife returned to the apartment at the afternoon's end.

'Guess who I spotted near the Sutro Baths?' I asked cheerfully.

'What,' she cried, 'are you spying on me now? Do you intend to control everything in my life, even those brief moments when I am out of your sight? If you want to know the truth, I'm beginning to feel as though I'm being stalked, like those bloody animals you photograph so relentlessly!'

'I wasn't following you,' I objected, 'though I've often been tempted. Sometimes I need to see you, just to confirm my good fortune and your continuing existence.'

'Don't worry about that,' she replied, 'my granny lived till she was ninety. I expect to do the same.'

After that she insisted I keep my distance from the institute where she worked. 'I need some space to call my own,' she explained. I respected her wishes, only to be castigated for showing no interest in her work.

'I've got some great news,' she announced, at the end of an otherwise regular day. 'I've been invited to attend a conference . . .'

'Congratulations,' I said.

'That's not the point,' she snapped. 'The point is the guest of honour. Guess who it is . . .'

'You tell me,' I replied.

'Only Bruno Bettelheim,' she said triumphantly.

'Great,' I replied.

'Is that all you can say?' she said. 'I thought you might like to accompany me. But obviously I was wrong.'

On the afternoon of her departure for the Uses of Enchantment weekend I began to have regrets. I found my wife in the bathroom. It was steamy. Floaters of talc glittered in the air. She was standing on a towel, pubic hair lightly dusted with Johnson's baby powder. Armpits damp with deodorant. I stole a kiss from that Aladdin's cave of hidden pheromones. But the sweetness was short-lived; my mouth became dry, as if I had bitten deeply into an unripe persimmon.

'Must you go?' I said, as she began to dress, each item increasing the distance between us.

She went, of course, and returned much later than

expected on the Sunday. I was watching a rerun of
She Wore a Yellow Ribbon when my wife re-entered
the apartment. I did not ask her why she was so late.
She offered no apologies and went straight to our
bedroom. A year or so passed before an explanation
finally emerged from an unexpected quarter.

There were insignificant earthquakes in or around
the city nearly every month. One such, triggered by
minor friction in the local fault line, caused all our
books both tragical and comical to dance the conga.
Clinging to my armchair I watched helplessly as
volume after volume shuffled from the dusty shelves,
including an entire set of the *Encyclopaedia Britannica*.
In the beginning an apple had sufficed; later whole
forests were required to contain our collective wisdom.
This was not advancement; it was arboricide. Either
way, knowledge was scattered all over our floor. Elsewhere crockery was being shattered in the kitchen,
giving the impression that a titanic domestic row was
in progress. Pictures dropped throughout the apartment, as though its walls had suddenly become
deciduous. One such was the glassy-eyed portrait of
my wife I just showed you. Its hanging had been the
occasion of some controversy. She had assured me that
she didn't object to her breasts being photographed,
so what harm in displaying the result?

My wife saw plenty. 'It makes me feel like I'm some
kind of a trophy,' she cried furiously. 'Why don't you

be honest and have me stuffed, mounted, and hung over the fireplace?'

'We don't have a fireplace,' I replied.

Later, she relented, and the picture went up. She's had the last word as usual (I thought), as I gingerly removed the cut-throat splinters that jealously protected her modesty. Inevitably the photograph shifted, thereby revealing a second image beneath. The subject was the same, with one notable difference.

My wife was posing in a shower stall, beneath a streaming cascade. Arms outstretched, breasts as glossy as toffee apples, pubic hair foamy with soap. Yes, pubic hair! The forbidden tuft resembled a goatee thick with shaving cream. It was a shameless performance, clearly put on for the exclusive benefit of the cameraman. Who was? If not her husband, then presumably her lover. Oh, I was a cuckold, of that there was no doubt. The wedding ring (easily visible amid the splayed fingers) supplied the incontrovertible dendrochronology. A more exhaustive scrutiny of the print (a shiny half-plate from Fotomart) revealed a complimentary bottle of shampoo discarded on the floor. Even closer examination (with a magnifying glass) disclosed the name of the hotel. I remembered instantly that my wife had stayed there with a couple of colleagues (let's call them Andersen and Grimm) when paying court to the great Bettelheim.

The radio reassured its audience that it had been a

small quake, with no fatalities. By the time my wife returned from her beloved institute, all the external damage had been repaired. Only residents and regular visitors would notice a few minor adjustments (even improvements) that the tremor had prompted. I was certain that my wife had registered the most significant instantly, precisely because it had rendered her speechless.

'An admirable piece of work,' I said at length. 'Would you mind revealing the name of the photographer?'

She obviously did.

'I assume that it is either Andersen or Grimm,' I said.

She was trapped. The camera couldn't lie; nor could she. She owned up to fucking the former twice; once in a meadow, once (later that same day) in the hotel (where they had shared a room). 'I'm so sorry,' she said.

I asked her to describe the meadow.

'The blades of the grass were unusually thick and slightly moist at the root,' she replied. 'There were a lot of wild flowers: buttercups, poppies, orchids, and goodness knows what else. At the centre was a stand of silver birch. We headed for it.'

'Is that where you dropped your knickers?'

'That's where I dropped my knickers.'

'Was it a good fuck?'

'It was a very good fuck.'

I bet it was. My wife was a passionate amateur; every fuck a bespoke fuck.

'Did he make you come?'

'No, though he thought he did.'

'Why did he think that?'

'I suppose it was because I made so much noise.'

'You always were a noisy screw.'

'I understand. I have hurt you. Now you want to hurt me.'

'How long did the affair last?'

'It was hardly an affair. More like a one-night stand.'

'Were you in love?'

'Call it an enchantment.'

'Are you still in touch, now that Andersen works in a distant city?'

'Yes.'

'How?'

'By letter.'

'What do you write?'

'I tell him about his former colleagues.'

'Is that all?'

'I add the odd endearment.'

'Such as?'

'Do you really want to know?'

'I wouldn't have asked if I didn't.'

'Well, I recently told him that I think of him every time I see a silver birch.'

I don't suppose this was strictly true, but it conclus-
ively besmirched my enjoyment of the Ansel Adams
landscape displayed in my studio. From that moment
I no longer saw slender silver birches, but rather the
limbs of lovers copulating wildly on a bed of chloro-
phyll. The informed heart had cracked.

•

My revenge was to shoot my wife, pubic hair and all.
Having had her modesty exposed as a sham, she was
in no position to protest as my camera roamed above,
between, below . . . I required her to assume provoca-
tive poses more typical of anxious-to-please starlets:
hands in hair, breasts shamelessly displayed, lips
parted and wet, eyes closed in ecstatic anticipation.
What was the alternative? A *crime passionnel*?

Most of these photographs were taken in motels.
One such – a cliff-top retreat near Big Sur – had a
sign beside its pool saying: 'Clothes Optional.' My wife
chose to take the option, wearing a one-piece swim-
suit redder than a virgin's blush, unlike the only other
sun-worshipper. That nameless beauty was unstitched
from top to toe.

'Why don't you follow her example?' I enquired.

'Because her breasts are bigger, and more beautiful,'
she replied. 'Besides, I don't want to risk skin cancer.'

I was disappointed; for some perverse reason I
wanted passing strangers to feast their eyes upon

my wife's nakedness. Who knows why? Ignoring my suggestion she draped a towel across a vacant mattress, then rinsed beneath an alfresco shower, accidentally reviving an image best forgotten.

'I bet you would have removed your costume if Andersen had asked,' I said, tasting bitter gall where there had been only sweetness.

My wife stood very still, as if I had slapped her. And then she was gone. The pool swallowed her whole. Simultaneously the woman on the sunbed sat up, attached a brassiere around her midriff, and slowly inched it into place. Having secured her breasts she rose to her feet and stepped into her knickers.

'You drove her away,' I said to my wife when she finally came up for air, 'Your false modesty made her uncomfortably aware of her nakedness.'

'Bullshit,' she replied, treading water, 'you eroticized an otherwise innocent situation. Do you think she didn't know that you were staring at her? You made her feel self-conscious. You embarrassed her. As you have embarrassed me.' She swam lap after lap until the sun dissolved into the ocean like a lemon sorbet melting on blue china.

Its glow filled our room, whose walls were hewn from the trunks of cedar. 'Now will you take the bloody thing off?' I said. Obligingly my wife hooked her thumbs beneath the shoulder straps and slowly began to unpeel the costume, as though flaying herself. Once it was free of the crotch it slipped down the remainder of her length as smoothly as a soul bound for Hades. When it crumpled at her ankles she lifted it with her right foot and lofted it aside. My wife was naked and radiant, a Joan of Arc on her pyre of logs.

'What next?' she asked, as she laid out the dress (still in its polythene sheath) she planned to wear for dinner. A dilemma: would it be life or art, a fuck or a photograph? No contest. The available light, that *ignis fatuus*, was simply too insistent to ignore. It cried, '*Carpe diem.*' And I seized what was left of it.

'Lie down,' I said.

'On the bed?' she asked.

'No,' I said, 'the floor.'

It was made of varnished wooden bricks, patterned with rings and starbursts. Honey-coloured. Almost an exact match for her lightly tanned skin.

'Back or front?' she asked.

'Face up,' I replied. Not that I intended to reproduce her face. Flat out on the king-size, old Olympus to my eye, I slithered forward like a big-game hunter (pushing aside my bunched-up jumper), not stopping until I had cut off my wife's head. I was equally anxious to exclude the window, through which the light poured, wanting to create the illusion that her body was a luminous object, a full moon in a darkened room. With her well-formed torso, blanched limbs, and perfect breasts – so straight, so immobile, so immutable – she certainly could have passed for the recumbent representation of some lunar goddess. Perhaps it was this statue-like quality that gave me the willies; made me feel that the real person had absconded. No prizes for guessing with whom. Try as I might it seemed that I couldn't remove from my mind what had come to pass beneath those indifferent silver birches. Instead of glorying in my wife's beauty I felt I would be better occupied in dusting the whole caboodle for signs of my rival's fingerprints.

But it wasn't me who eventually punished her. It wasn't me who placed the lump in her left breast before the year was out. 'It's probably a benign cyst,' said Surgeon A, after examining the afflicted appendage. Then he said it probably wasn't, having noted spots of microcalcification on the mammogram.

'My dear,' he said, after the abnormality had been removed and declared malignant, 'I have two things to tell you. The first is that the tumour has been excised, and will never kill you. The other thing I must tell you is that the cells around the site – and this surprised me – are precancerous. I double-checked to make sure, my dear, but I'm afraid there is no doubt. The problem is not immediately life-threatening, but you must consider treating it, lest it become so. You understand, my dear?'

'I think you want my breast,' replied my wife.

'Not necessarily,' said Surgeon A, 'though it is the most likely option.'

As we left his oak-panelled consulting rooms he patted my wife's head. 'It is a tragedy,' he said, 'but not a serious one.'

Surgeon A measured the tumour at 4 mm, and classed it as grade 1. Surgeon B said the tumour was 7.7 mm and grade 2. Surgeon A recommended a mastectomy. Surgeon B proposed an intermediary procedure. Surgeon A was not flattered by the second opinion.

'My dear,' he complained, 'your johnny-come-lately spends most of his time in Boston looking down test tubes. He's never had a moment of common sense in his entire life. Whereas I practically live in the operating theatre. And I am promising you a complete recovery. What more do you want?' he paused. 'Why won't you trust me?' he asked.

'It's not that I didn't trust him,' my wife explained afterwards. 'I simply thought that his speech contained too many flourishes. I favour a surgeon with a sharper tongue.'

Given the green light, Surgeon B operated immediately. He set about removing all the suspect tissue from the left breast, as well as several lymph nodes from the adjoining armpit. For several days the fate of my wife's sinister tit remained suspended in the brassiere of fate. The verdict was delivered in a stark consulting room.

The good news was that the lymph nodes were clean, indicating that the cancer had not spread; the bad news was that the breast was infiltrated beyond redemption. 'Unfortunately we were forced to leave too many cells that were mammographically occult,' admitted Surgeon B, 'all of them fully capable of forming tumours by stealth.' Obviously the nest of vipers had to go. By way of compensation Surgeon B suggested a simultaneous reconstruction.

He rose from his desk and beckoned my wife to follow him. They disappeared behind a screen.

I heard him say: 'May I have a look at the breasts?' My wife obviously obliged, because I heard him ask: 'What are you? A D-cup?'

'You have a good eye,' she said.

'And you have nice breasts,' he replied. 'It is a pity that you must sacrifice one of them.'

'Thank you,' she said.

'There is some ptosis evident in both,' he continued. 'You understand that the replacement will not possess the elastic properties of its natural twin. A silicone implant – which can be inflated or deflated as you see fit – will help. But the match will never be perfect. Nor will the prosthesis be blessed with a nipple.'

'Whatever it looks like it will be better than nothing,' said my wife.

At the appointed hour Surgeon B (dapper in a charcoal suit) asked my wife to remove her hospital gown and perch on the end of her bed. Whereupon he picked up his tape-measure and began to dictate to his assistant: 'Inter-nipple distance is 22 cm . . . midline crease is 8.5 cm on left . . . projection is 4 cm on either side.' Having gathered the requisite data he seized his magic marker and outlined an imaginary brassiere across my wife's bare chest. Amputation was the easy bit. Rebuilding would be much harder. In order to secure the silicone implant it was necessary to move a dorsal muscle – literally – back to front. This too was marked with black ink. As was a patch of skin shaped like a pear or a large teardrop. Then came the porter with a gurney.

I followed, permission having been obtained from Surgeon B to photograph the proceedings. My wife had been horrified when I first mooted the possibility.

'Are you a sicko,' she cried, 'or simply mad?'

'Both are distinct possibilities,' I replied, 'though the fact that I love you is another consideration. If I could I would be your pain-bearer. As it is the best I can do is be near you.'

I guess I said the right thing, because my wife kissed me.

'Besides,' I added, 'there's a certain symmetry involved. I first saw your left breast through one view-finder, and I'll say goodbye to it through another.'

We paused at an antechamber. From my distance it seemed as though the anaesthetist had cast a spell over my wife: one moment she was waving at me, the next she was in a wide-eyed stupor. As the silent porter wheeled the gurney into the operating theatre itself a cluster of nurses split apart, scattering like startled deer. They quickly regrouped around the supine form of my unconscious wife. One disposed of her hospital gown, revealing the entire length of her body. Another raised her limp left arm and carefully shaved the exposed armpit. A third, masked and gloved, took centre stage. She picked up a small envelope, from which she removed something that resembled a pocket handkerchief. This she dipped in a stainless steel bowl brimming with a disinfectant which just happened to be the colour of blood. Using the drenched gauze the masked nurse began to paint my wife's left breast, starting at the nipple and moving outwards in con-centric circles until the whole breast was the colour of blood. Opening another envelope she did the same for the armpit and upper arm. Finally she stepped back and removed her rubber gloves, as if she were a magician's assistant whose job it was to prepare a volunteer from the audience for some unspecified wizardry. And then the magician himself entered the expectant theatre, dressed in a priestly robe of opal green. He nodded in my direction, the first to acknow-ledge my presence.

He spoke so quickly I could barely hear him. It soon became apparent that he had demanded towels. He placed four of them around my wife's offered breast. 'Clips,' he said. Then, 'Drape.' At which the attendant nurses covered my wife with linen sheets, so that the condemned breast alone was presented through a rectangular opening. I saw all this through the viewfinder of my Olympus. I also saw Surgeon B gather the scalpel and draw a line around the base of my wife's breast, as he had done previously with the magic marker. That done, he leaned over his patient, and all was hidden from my gaze save his overarching back. When he stepped away I could see clearly enough that the breast was no longer there. In its place was a gaping wound, a shining patch of red and yellow. The breast itself was cupped in his hands. I heard a muffled echo as he dropped it into a cardboard box. It was enough. I turned, horror-struck, and fled the theatre. Not because I was nauseated and dreaded to see more, but because I had begun to feel the unmistakable nudgings of arousal in my pants. No one observed my departure.

When my wife was restored to the ward some four hours later, she had five drains for her wounds, two drips, and an oxygen supply attached to her nose. 'It might not look very likely now,' said Surgeon B, 'but her prognosis is excellent. A ninety per cent chance of old age.'

My wife was grateful to the medical team for saving her life, but was not impressed by my photographs of them in action. 'I look like I'm posing for Les Krims,' was all she would say. As soon as her wounds had healed she made her way back to her favourite purveyors of lingerie, now vulgarized with a storefront and a name. 'To prove that I am still a woman,' as she put it. I accompanied her as far as Union Square.

'We'll meet again in an hour,' I said, as she turned right into Maiden Lane, and I entered the headquarters of *Pays Inconnu*.

'Hot enough for you?' asked Angelika Ikon, observing that even my sweatshirt was sweating.

'Apparently it's the hottest March day in the city's history,' I said, repeating what I had caught on the radio.

'I was sorry to hear about your wife,' said Angelika Ikon. 'How is she doing?'

'Much better,' I replied. 'In fact she's around the corner, splashing out on new underwear.'

'Good for her,' said Angelika Ikon, summoning her secretary. 'Check out our box of Celestial Seasonings,' she said to the young woman, who (as far as I could see) was wearing a tight cotton dress and nothing else, 'and pick something refreshing. Our guest needs cooling down.'

I shifted uncomfortably in my seat, aware of the picture editor's disapproval. But how could I help eyeballing her minion? How could I resist animal instinct?

'I have often wondered,' asked Angelika Ikon, 'what

turned a man of your obvious predilections on to wildlife photography?'

'Birds,' I replied. 'The feathered kind. When I was
a kid I loved to watch them land in the park or on the
beach. To me they were all UFOs. I didn't know an
oriole from a cardinal. But I loved them just the same.
Eventually I learned to name them. Inevitably I wanted
to possess them too. But it was not possible. My
mother was extremely superstitious, and believed that
birds indoors brought bad luck. I had to capture them
some other way. It never occurred to me to record their
sound. Probably because I always valued seeing over
hearing, being tone-deaf. Besides, birdsong often refers
to something other than the singer; as in, "Hail to
thee, blithe Spirit! Bird thou never wert . . ." No, I
wanted a good camera. My father – who needed little
persuading – replaced my old Brownie with a Yashica.
I finished my first roll in an afternoon. In those days
you had to wait a whole week for the prints to come
back from the processors. What a disappointment!
Where were the birds? Practically invisible. Mere
specks in the air. Obviously I needed to get much
closer. But how? In short, I was tutored by my errors.'

'How about their perches?' said Angelika Ikon. 'Are
they also of interest?'

'You mean trees?'

'Not just any trees,' she said. 'I mean the Bristlecone
Pines. Are you familiar with them?'

'Naturally,' I replied. 'The oldest living things on God's earth. Confined to the American south-west; most particularly the White Mountains.'

'I'd like you to take some nice pictures of them,' said Angelika Ikon. 'Standard fee. Usual generous expenses. You like the sound of it?'

Back in the street I waited for my wife beside a mime artist masquerading as a robot, his essential humanity exposed by the involuntary perspiration that dribbled down his cheeks. Nor could he do anything about the glass moustache that had sprouted above his upper lip. When my wife eventually appeared, carrying a bag marked 'Iodoform Kate's', I dropped a dollar bill into his hat. It wasn't the money that moved him, but my wife's resurrected cleavage. 'Wow,' he mouthed.

'Well, it's certainly changed a bit since my mother's day,' she said. 'Apparently Kate was an infamous tart who worked the Lane. You'd think I was applying to be her replacement, the way the sales assistant sized me up. Changed her tune, of course, when she saw my tits. In fact she pressed a small gift upon me.'

My wife handed me a little box with the words 'Nearly Me Nipples' embossed upon it. Within was a replica nipple, backed with a suction pad, not unlike the tip of a toy arrow. Surely the time-honoured badge of the the Society of the Amazons.

'I'm sporting another,' said my wife, 'beneath my new two-hundred-dollar bra.'

'It's a good thing that Angelika Ikon's just given me a job,' I replied.

•

'The White Mountains are on the far side of the state,' I explained. 'To reach them it's necessary to cross the Central Valley. Would you care to keep me company?'

'I've been away from work too long already,' she said. 'Maybe in a few months. If the magazine can wait.'

'Why not?' I said. 'The trees have been there for five thousand years. They aren't going anywhere in a hurry.'

In the meantime I had the old Impala serviced, to be on the safe side. I also took the opportunity of having the ancient dent in the wing smoothed over. We set off in September, and expected to be away for a week.

On the first day we drove south, through drifting banks of coastal fog; ocean to the right, fields of artichokes or Brussels sprouts to the left. Buzzards perched on telegraph poles, waiting to make the call all rodents dread. At Big Basin the fog lifted sufficiently to reveal a ferocious feeding frenzy, a one-sided sea-battle between fish and fowl. I hit the brakes and grabbed my cameras. Ran to the beach and stood in the eye-watering wind as banners of silk formed ever-changing curlicues in the cloudless sky. Even as I watched, the flags were ripped from the heavens and hurled down towards the depths below. As they fell they disintegrated, were transformed into innumerable black-hatted terns that fizzed into the roiling surf. The helpless anchovies must have felt like the French at Agincourt. And the terns were merely the first wave. Packs of screaming gulls followed them, plunging pell-mell into the unquiet waters. Then came the heavy artillery: pelicans patrolling the agitated surface in twos and threes – a dozen wing beats, then a long glide until the quarry was spotted. Whereupon these latter-day dodos performed a balletic volte-face and plummeted headlong into the boil like thunderbolts. Scores of other birds scavenged upon the sands, shrieking at rivals intent upon picking at their booty. Weather, water, wildlife – all at full pitch; even the denizens of pandemonium would have considered it noisy.

Consequently I did not hear my wife when she called my name. The first thing I saw was a trembling chick cradled in her arms, one of the few avian casualties of the massacre. It looked like a small penguin, save that its beak was long and dark. A murre, then. A murre that was wearing an overcoat of oil. The poor creature was too weak to do anything other than emit a plaintive one-note whimper.

'We must save it,' said my wife, who was of the opinion – long held – that every living creature was redeemable. It was my unpleasant duty to disabuse her.

'Francis of Assisi himself couldn't do that,' I said, taking a close-up of the stricken murre's unblinking eye; a pinhead of amber on a feathery field of black snow.

'At least let it die in peace,' she said.

Ignoring her request I continued to record its last moments.

'Are you really such a heartless bastard?' asked my wife. 'Is it really necessary to turn this little thing's death agonies into art?'

Why was she so upset? Was she warning me not to do the same to her, should the cancer return with a vengeance? Whatever the reason, I thought better of trying to explain that my camera was a kind of safety net in which I tried to catch the living before they fell from this world.

My wife washed the oil from her hands at Nepenthe. Nepenthe has three definitions: first, the former love nest of Rita Hayworth and Orson Welles; second, a restaurant on the same site; third, a drug that induces forgetfulness of grief. Perhaps the waiter (a pickled hippie from Haight-Ashbury), slipped some in her cappuccino. Certainly she brightened sufficiently to order lunch. From our table beside the window we could observe the vertiginous sweep of the coast and, in the foreground, broiling blue jays gasping open-beaked on the branches of live oaks. The day had turned hotter than a Habanero pepper.

'I'm glad I decided to come,' she said.

'Me too,' I replied, as the food arrived.

Her lamb was laid out like a winning hand of cards. The vegetables, wrapped in slices of courgette and topped with a headdress of rosemary, were mounted on a spiral staircase of potato slices. The whole looked like it was meant to be hung rather than eaten. I was served red snapper, followed by persimmon pudding with a dash of Chantilly cream. Slipping seductively from the silver spoon it sweet-talked my taste buds and generally created a pleasant internal environment, marred only by the afterburn of infidelity and illness.

•

'Remind me what your wife does,' requests Angelika Ikon.

'She's a secular nun, a sister of the order of St Bruno,' I reply. 'Her job is to bring the word to society's damaged goods.'

'You sound bitter,' she observes, 'as if you think she's giving too much of herself to her work.' Or to her fellow workers. I bite my tongue, but I cannot contain my emotion. 'Are you all right?' asks Angelika Ikon. 'You've started to shiver.'

'It's no wonder,' I reply. 'My shoes and socks are drenched, and my feet are beginning to freeze.'

In the absence of a St Bernard, I order a third grappa from our snarling waitress.

'I don't blame you for being so bad-tempered,' says Angelika Ikon to the half-naked young woman, 'your tits must be turning to ice. Why don't you just refuse to wear that degrading outfit? Surely you realize that in advertising your own availability, you are endangering all of us?'

'I'll tell you why,' she replies. 'I can't get work as an actress, and I need the fucking money. When it comes down to it, I'd rather be raped than starve.' So saying she turns her shapely back upon her would-be saviour.

'Your wife must have the patience of a saint,' says Angelika Ikon. 'Who are these people she helps? Who exactly are society's damaged goods?'

'Disgruntled waitresses, drug addicts, prostitutes, the prematurely pregnant,' I reply, 'but mainly maladjusted adolescent males.'

'At last!' exclaims my companion. 'The mystery of her interest in you is explained!'

The waitress returns, and bangs the grappa down in front of me. 'Will that be all?' she asks.

Although the windows of the café are weeping with condensation, they are sufficiently transparent for me to make out the flickering silhouette of an ascending

pedestrian. 'I think I'll take my chances outside,' I say
to Angelika Ikon. 'I need to get into some dry clothes
before pneumonia sets in.'

'I'll accompany you as far as Stockton and Bay,' she
replies.

We leave the comforts afforded by electricity, and
enter the newly-minted wilderness. Only to find that
the bellicose wind has ceased, and the snow-bearing
clouds dispersed, to reveal a moon as brilliant as
burnished platinum. This, in turn, illuminates a spell-
bound cityscape. The only sounds come from our own
lungs. The rest is silence. It is as though our familiar
metropolis has sloughed off its former skin to reveal
the crystalline purity beneath, the white surface on
which a new and better history will be written, starting
from tomorrow.

Thanks to the fact that Angelika Ikon had the fore-
sight to slip into her mother's old golf shoes (spike-
soled like the old battleaxe), we make excellent
progress. At the entrance to her building Angelika Ikon
kisses me on the cheek and says: 'You might like to
know that your admirable studies of the Bristlecone
Pines will be appearing in the February issue of *Pays
Inconnu.*'

•

San Francisco, under snow, may look other-worldly,
but it is nowhere near as alien as the other side of the

Central Valley, a godforsaken land of parallel lines that beckon you ever nearer the vanishing point.

Except that the vanishing point kept vanishing. Unable to disappear, we did the next best thing and checked into the Happy Trails Motel. The proprietor looked strangely familiar, something to do with his powder-blue shirt and matching pants.

'How come this place is called Lone Pine?' asked my wife, prickly after a day dominated by sand and cacti. 'I haven't seen a single tree.'

'There used to be one, ma'am,' he replied, 'but not any more. Got washed away in a flood. Or so they claim.'

'Are you a local?' I asked.

'No, sir,' he replied, 'I'm from Hollywood.' He paused. 'I used to be the Lone Ranger.'

My heart skipped a beat. 'Surely you're not Clayton Moore?' I asked.

'No, sir,' he said, 'nor John Hart either.'

'Then how can you call yourself the Lone Ranger?' I demanded.

'Perhaps not *the* Lone Ranger,' he conceded, 'but certainly *a* Lone Ranger. For the sake of my good name I'll explain the distinction. The Lone Ranger used to wear a mask, as you know. This was very convenient. It meant that any actor could play the part. Especially in long-shot. Many was the time that I galloped off with a hearty "Hi-yo, Silver!", while Clayton Moore sipped coffee in his trailer. He was happy and so was I. I fell in love with a good woman, and decided to spend the rest of my days here. It may not be Holly-wood, but to me it's been Paradise.'

While my wife soaked in the bath I unpacked the Olympus and a tripod and went back in search of the Lone Ranger. I needed to obtain his portrait to have some external proof of his existence.

'If you'd prefer,' he said, clearly rather moved by my suggestion, 'you can have one of these stills. I've plenty in the office. I'll even autograph it if you like.'

He picked up a framed photograph and tapped the glass with a bent finger. 'My one and only close-up,' he said proudly. He was on horseback, and reaching for the sky. Two men, armed with rifles, but obviously exhausted, were leaning against a giant boulder. They were both pointing their guns at him.

'It ain't what it appears,' he explained. 'They are a couple of besieged prospectors. They hear a horseman approach. "Our number's up," they think. They prepare to fight to the death. Then they recognize the figure riding towards them. "Don't shoot, it's the Lone Ranger!" they cry in relief. That single sentence has justified my entire life.'

'I'd be honoured to accept it, *kemo sabe*,' I said.

'If you're interested I can show you exactly where the programmes were made,' he said, selecting a map from the rack on the wall and unfolding it on his desk.

'These are the Alabama Hills,' he continued, 'location of a thousand Westerns. John Wayne worked up there, as did Humphrey Bogart, Errol Flynn, Randolph Scott, Clint Eastwood, the whole crew. Not to mention your host. His happy hunting ground, Lone Ranger Canyon, is about a fifteen-minute drive from here.'

He refolded the map and handed it to me.

'Since you're obviously a keen cameraman,' he added, 'you shouldn't leave the area without taking a turn around Picture Rocks Circle. It's got photo opportunities you wouldn't believe: outcrops of granite that resemble bears, baboons, knights in armour, spooks, elephants, eagles, you name it. There's even one that's the spitting image of Batman. So lifelike you'd swear he was breathing. Everyone agrees, it's a fabulous attraction.'

He looked at his watch.

'I always have a drink at this hour,' he said. 'Perhaps you would care to join me?'

We sat out on the porch while a whirligig of bugs made merry in the twilight, as if they were weaving a tapestry of stars. The whiskey glowed in our glass like little suns, which set in our bellies. We drank our way through several days.

'I think you are the only happy man I've ever met,' I said, on the third or fourth.

'If you mean I don't want more than I've got,' he said, 'then I agree, I'm a happy man.'

'Tell me,' I said, on the seventh, 'what would you do if you ever found out that your wife had been unfaithful?'

'I'd shoot myself,' he said.

'Not her?' I asked.

'Nope,' he replied, 'I wouldn't want to live with the knowledge of my wife's betrayal.'

'I do,' I said, shocking myself. I hadn't told anyone about my wife's infidelity before. I could hardly bear to repeat it to myself.

'How do you feel?' he asked.

'Like you would if Tonto ran off with the Range Rider.'

'You poor bastard,' he said, squeezing my shoulder with an arthritic hand.

Darkness fell upon the Alabama Hills, but sleep would not follow. To start with our room was too hot. Then the air conditioner wheezed and chattered like a polar bear rattling its cage.

'Are you awake?' whispered my wife conspiratorially.

I grunted affirmatively.

'Good,' she said, 'good.' Then she added: 'Do you feel up to buggering me?'

She didn't need to ask twice. Unfortunately, sodomy is not as easy as it looks. The black hole in her posterior would have had trouble accommodating a rectal thermometer.

'It's no use,' I said, 'we need some lubrication.'

I ransacked the bathroom.

'Perhaps shampoo will do the trick,' I called.

'I don't think so,' said my wife, still on all fours. 'I don't want to blow bubbles every time I break wind.'

Eventually, walking past the breakfast tray, I spied a pat of margarine. First I parted her cheeks, then I spread the yellow goo. It did the trick.

'I can't believe it's not butter,' gasped my wife, as I finally gained entry. Pausing at base camp, I found my equilibrium.

'What does it feel like?' she enquired.

'Like I'm wearing a wedding ring on my dick,' I replied.

'That's nice,' she said.

'Tell me,' I said, 'why tonight after all these years?'

'Because of how you were this afternoon,' she said. 'You were so excited when the innkeeper introduced himself as the Lone Ranger. Just like a little boy. It made me want to give you a present too.'

As I probed deeper into my wife's innards, blood began to trickle from where I had accidentally engineered a minor episiotomy.

'Do you want me to stop?' I asked.

'No, go on.'

So I proceeded to bore into her rump.

'Deeper,' she insisted, 'go deeper.'

'I'm up to my balls already,' I replied.

'There was another reason,' whispered my wife. 'I thought that if I gave you a part of myself no one else had ever had it would help you forget about Andersen.'

I withdrew a little, then rammed my stiff cock into her with all my might.

'That's it, my love, that's it!' she cried. 'I want you to split me in two!'

By now the blood was flowing freely from her anus, but I was too far gone to care. Nor did I pay any attention to her sobs and unrestrained screams. As I have said, she always was a noisy fuck. However, I stopped soon enough when I saw the masked man with silver six-guns in either hand. Both pointing at me.

'Don't fret, ma'am, you're safe now,' he said, 'the Lone Ranger is here.'

My wife collapsed beneath me, laughing hysterically.

'Now let her be, you murdering bastard,' he added, with uncharacteristic vulgarity, brandishing his anachronistic weapons.

'Why are you here, you blundering oaf?' squealed my wife. 'This man is my husband, and he was doing nothing more criminal than enjoying his conjugal rights, albeit in an unorthodox fashion.'

He wavered, but had spotted the blood stains on the sheets and remained unconvinced.

My wife stood up. Her body was glazed with sweat.

All she cared to cover, I noted, was the locum tenens on her chest. 'Do I look like the victim of a violent assault?' she asked.

'Oh Lord,' wailed the Lone Ranger, 'what have I done?'

Seeing his distress, I said (while rapidly pulling on my pants): 'Better to have made such a mistake than to have found a corpse in the morning. When my wife has calmed down I'm sure she will recognize the valour of your action.'

'To tell you the truth, it was my wife who sent me over,' moaned the Lone Ranger, 'having become convinced by all the available evidence that you were butchering yours. I assured her that you weren't the type. But then I remembered the confidences we shared over those sundowners, and I wasn't quite so assured. Obviously I should have trusted my first impression.'

My shameless wife, having wrapped herself in a towel, said: 'It's a thin line between heroics and buffoonery. Tonight you ended on the wrong side. I wish you better luck next time.'

'There won't be a next time,' replied the Lone Ranger. 'As to this time, I'd be grateful if it went no further than this room. The Wrather Corporation, who own the franchise, have decided that the Lone Ranger of the future will be a handsome young buck called Klinton Spilsbury, and they don't take kindly to old-timers donning the mask. They even took poor Clayton Moore to court and had him stripped of the right to wear it. So you can imagine what they would do to me.'

'Don't worry,' I said, 'your secret's safe with us.'

'His, maybe,' said my wife, as soon as we were alone, 'but how about mine? What exactly did you tell him over the Jack Daniel's?'

'I told him about your problem with the truth,' I said.

'That's a very grand way of describing such a mundane event,' she said.

'If only I could think of it as such,' I said.

'But why tell a stranger,' she said, 'rather than a friend or – God forbid – a shrink?'

'He isn't a stranger,' I said, 'he's the Lone Ranger. I've known him all my life. He belongs to those thrilling – and secure – days of yesteryear, when television was black and white, and so was everything else.'

'Who are you kidding?' she said. 'He's nothing but a tenth-rate actor living on past glories. And a liar. His wife didn't send him. He'd been listening outside our door. What else was that stethoscope for?'

•

'From Lone Pine to Big Pine via Independence. Then on to Bishop. At Bishop we began our ascent of the White Mountains, until we reached our goal: the ancient stands of the Bristlecones. Even then we had further to travel, for the most photogenic grew in Patriarch Grove, across a dozen more miles of dirt, on one of the highest mesas in the country. We arrived trailing clouds of dust and left the Impala steaming in the thin air. The sky seemed close enough to touch, as blue and as perfect as a divine iris. Pre-dating Abraham, many of the blasted and contorted trees remained fertile, producing cones annually. One of which my wife plucked, notwithstanding all prohibitions to the contrary.

'What have you done?' I cried.

'Don't be such a fusspot,' she replied. 'A cone more or less will make no difference up here, but will mean a great deal in my place of work. The tree which produced it was already old when the Greeks attacked Troy, even older when the Hebrew slaves built the pyramids in Egypt. It was distinctly venerable when Antony fell for Cleopatra. And well over four thousand when the Civil War began. You get the idea. Kids with no future will be converted into optimists by this cone. We will plant its seeds and watch them grow for as long as we are able, knowing that we have sent a message to posterity.'

I went about my business photographing the trees, carefully framing their golden boughs against the uncluttered sky. I continued until clouds began to obscure the sun. The valley below darkened, and the

snow on the surrounding peaks turned lustreless. A
cold wind started to blow, driving ice crystals before
it. I turned and began to descend in the direction of
my wife. Her voice beat against the wind like an invisible bird. Its cry I soon realized was: 'Save me! Save
me!' From what? Of course I couldn't run at such an
altitude, but I walked as briskly as I was able. As I
approached it gradually became clear that my wife
was standing, but equally clear that she was in great
distress. She had been stripped to the buff. Literally.
Not a single hair remained on her body. Seeing me
she stretched out her arms, but seemed incapable of
further movement, not even to shield herself from the
fierce shower of snow, the first of the new season.

The reason soon became apparent. Her toenails had
grown as long as talons and rooted themselves in the
scree. 'My back! My back!' she whimpered. Then: 'I
can't bear it! I can't bear it!' I could hear the bones
cracking within her. Her flesh began to shrivel and
harden; her skin wrinkled and darkened, grew more
arborescent by the moment. Bark bound her legs into
a single trunk; it overlaid her lap, corseted her hips.
She gasped as it corked her sex. Nor did it cease there.
The bark rose until it had encrusted her breasts. Meanwhile her arms were changed into boughs. Her hands
withered until they were mere twigs. She opened her
mouth to speak, but the encroaching bark gagged
her. Her tongue emerged nonetheless, but hardened

into a knot as I watched. 'I love you,' I shouted, as the rough icing smothered her ears. 'I love you,' I repeated, knowing she would hear no further sound. A ragged blindfold put an end to her stream of gummy tears. And a crown of wood completed the enclosure. Her tears had solidified on the cold ground, become beads of amber. I gathered them instead. Words of comfort were harder to find. What could I say before departing, before abandoning my wife to the permafrost? 'At least you'll outlive me,' was the best I could do. Of a sudden the snow ceased, the clouds parted, and the incandescent sun instantly electroplated the upstart tree, so that its contorted boughs shone like a gilded brooch pinned to heaven's purple raiments. By good fortune there was an unfinished roll of Kodachrome in my Olympus.

If you look carefully at the photographs in the forthcoming issue of *Pays Inconnu* you may note in one or two of the shots an incongruous gold band around one of the smaller branches of a particular Bristlecone Pine. It is my wife's wedding ring.

ii

After the extraordinary incident that I can only call my wife's metamorphosis, I was overcome with a kind of vertigo, as if my feet were balanced precariously on the crest of a gigantic wave. But I waited in vain for its downward motion, for the ultimate rush as it hurtled me to earth, some eleven thousand feet below. Given what I had just witnessed it was not an improbable wish. Anything could happen in this, the most unstable state in the Union. It rested upon gilded splinters. Its inhabitants counted transformation as a birthright. They employed plastic surgeons to alter their bodies, psychiatrists to change their minds, priests to redirect their souls. Above all, there was Hollywood, the omphalos of transfiguration, where dross was turned to gold, Marion Morrison into John Wayne. And there were the White Mountains, where my lovely wife was changed into a tree.

Since the icy peak would not cast me off, I

descended of my own volition; down I went, down, down into Death Valley. My spirits sank with the road which finally touched bottom at Badwater, the lowest point in the western hemisphere. From there all exits were ascents, the only way out was up. Needless to say, I lacked the inclination for such a bullish gesture. In short, I was marooned in a spiritual doldrum.

The desert air shuddered with heat. Mirages took many forms, including that of a woman who shimmied enticingly at the side of the road. Her dress seemed to consist of nothing but sequins. Her face was a smudge. Was it my wife? What if the sequence in the forest had been an illusion, nothing but a symptom of altitude sickness? In which case the poor girl was probably out of resources and trying to hitch a ride home. I stuck my head out of the car window and felt the searing wind scorch my cheeks. 'Get in,' I shouted, 'I'm on my way to San Francisco.' Closer inspection revealed my folly. The mirage was nothing like my wife, was in fact nothing, a mere confection of hot air. Bereaved yet again I slumped over the steering wheel.

The sky marked the passage of time, changing from blood-orange to lemon, then from peppermint-green to midnight-blue. At an uncertain hour a flashlight progressed through the darkness. Was it the Lord, rounding up lost sheep? No, it came with a cop attached.

'You're alive,' he noted, when I raised my head. 'I was beginning to wonder.'

'Just doing a little soul-searching, officer,' I replied.

'When you've found what you're looking for,' he said, 'you might consider moving on. This ain't no camping ground.'

Where to? I flattened the road-map upon the vacant passenger seat and began to plot my gradual disappearance among the ghost towns of the Sierras. It was by no means impractical. I was, after all, less encumbered than the Lone Ranger. Who would miss me? No wife. My parents were deceased, as were my in-laws. Only Angelika Ikon would casually note my absence when I failed to deliver the pix on or about the deadline, and then think no more of me. It was a temptation: to cease to exist as a social being. To add my few portables to the detritus of the gold rush.

As night withdrew, the Black Mountains became distinct. Funeral Peak grew a halo. Across the featureless valley the Panamint Range developed a lavender blush. And then, at the aphelion of the Impala's giant shadow, I saw something tiptoe across the dun-coloured sand, something wearing a tawny coat. As if trained for the task, it daintily trod the borderline between dark and light, day and night. At some point it must have sensed my attention, for it suddenly paused midway and turned its face towards me.

Its ears were erect, on full alert, its mouth slightly

agape. We eyed each other like a pair of world-weary
gunslingers, the Death Valley Fox and I, old pros who
knew that the town wasn't big enough for the both of
us. But I had an unfair advantage. The newly-minted
sun was at my back, enabling me to outfox the fox.
Before it could move a muscle the Olympus was in my
hand. I managed three shots and then it was away,
loping out of the frame. By which time tears of gratitude occluded my vision. My vulpine saviour had
shown that there was still life in the old dog; that his
instincts were still sharp, and his shutter-finger still
itchy. Blessing the creature, I started the engine and
ascended the hill to civilization.

It is an unfortunate fact that when sap rather than
blood flows through a woman's veins, and her flesh is
no longer soft to the touch, all of her most feminine
accessories are rendered null and void. I knew that I
would have to sort out my wife's belongings as soon
as I returned to Lombard and Grant, before they could
assume the symbolic weight of sacred relics. I spared
nothing. Her myriad dresses stood to attention in the
wardrobe, like some phantom army, awaiting the call
to arms that would never come again. I scythed them
down with a single sweep of my forearm. That done
I turned my attention to her bras and panties, stored
en masse in an antique cabinet. I opened every one of
its drawers, and plunged my hand into the topmost,
expecting only unresisting silk, but receiving instead

a splinter from the untreated wood of its interior. As I extracted it with a hot needle and tweezers, I took some consolation from the fact that my wife had been transformed into a protected species, and had been spared the fate of the common redwood. Otherwise she might even now have been floating down some fast-flowing river *en route* to her destiny as an A-frame or – irony of ironies – a container for the undies that had once barely contained her.

Newly bandaged I returned to my labours and plucked out a handful of gorgeous pants, as flimsy and as colourful as tropical plumage. I pressed a cluster to my nose in hopes of scenting the wearer's ripeness in the gussets, but found only the anonymous whiff of detergent. I dumped them all into a large plastic sack. The brassieres – neatly laid out so that they resembled a box of tightly packed pears – were equally unmindful of their erstwhile occupant. They followed the knickers into the bag. I ransacked the last drawer, burrowed through its suspenders, stockings, and socks, until I touched something incongruous; something that felt like a mounted photograph.

What an unexpected treasure! It was to all appearances a black and white portrait of my wife, in the style of a *fin-de-siècle* pin-up. She was naked beneath a sheer black sheath sufficiently diaphanous to allow an unobstructed view of her breasts. And everything else too, for that matter. Excepting the privy parts,

which my still modest spouse-in-waiting was shielding
with her hands. She must have been about nineteen
or twenty, the precise time of our first intimacies. Since
I had no recollection of shooting the photograph, it
followed that it must have been the work of a hitherto
unknown rival. The word 'Kaloma' embossed in gothic
script on the bottom was the only clue as to his
identity. What was not in doubt was his talent. The
photograph was suffused with a milky light, so soft,
delicious, and pure it looked drinkable. The brightness
cascaded over my wife, creating the illusion that she
was glowing from within and seething with a vitality
that superseded the voluptuous. There was no ambi-
guity in her expression; here was yet more evidence
of her promiscuity.

That intemperate and hasty conclusion lasted only
for the time it took to turn the photograph over. Whereupon I received an even bigger shock. Stamped on the
reverse was the following: 'Copyright 1914 – PN CO'.
But if it wasn't my wife, who was it that bore such a
close resemblance to her? Had her orphaned granny
been a more colourful character than previously suspected? So many questions. But, alas, there was no
one left to answer.

After that manic assault upon my wife's clothing I
calmed down and began removing her possessions in
a more systematic manner. It is now February, and
I am all but done. Returning for the last time from the

medical foundation that is benefiting from her munificent wardrobe, I find Angelika Ikon awaiting me on my doorstep. She is holding a bag of shopping in one hand, and a bunch of flowers in the other.

'I can hardly believe what I have just heard about your wife,' she cries. 'Tell me it isn't true.'

'I only wish I could,' I say.

'I'm so sorry,' says Angelika Ikon. 'Is there anything I can do?'

'You can change the subject,' I reply.

'I understand,' says Angelika Ikon, handing me the flowers. But she can't. 'When we met in Tobaccus you must have been in such pain,' she says. 'And what did I do to ease it? Only accused you of being a femicide!'

'You weren't to know,' I say.

'But I should have seen that something was amiss,' she says, 'and I want to make amends for my insensitivity. I've a packet of Aidell's Hot Italian Sausages in my bag, as well as some rare arugula from Enrico's. It's nutty and sharp and, according to old Enrico, goes with the links like Jerry Lewis goes with Dean Martin. So how about letting me come upstairs and cook you dinner?'

I can think of no polite way to decline, so I unlock the front door and usher her into the lobby.

Angelika Ikon stands before the kitchen window, looking down upon Alcatraz and the Golden Gate Bridge. The window also provides access to a flat roof, a secluded suntrap which my wife transformed into a herb garden: basil, dill, coriander, rosemary, lavender, et cetera, et cetera, all in their individual terracotta pots. They survived the snow, which turned out to be a one-day wonder. Now they are growing abundantly, thanks to the warmth of an early spring.

'It's such a lovely afternoon,' says Angelika Ikon. 'Do you think we could have an aperitif out there?'

'Why not?' I say, plucking a maturing bottle of Le Cigare Volant from the rack. What else am I saving it for?

Angelika Ikon clambers through the window first. I pursue, heavy with a sense of *déjà vu*.

On warm summer evenings, my wife liked nothing better than to shed her clothes after work, climb through the very same window, and bake slowly and fragrantly on the hot asphalt. Once I caught her *in flagrante delicto*, spreadeagled, every orifice (down to the smallest pore) open to the sun, and made a beeline for my camera. Having sneaked several photos of my unwitting subject, I ditched the Olympus and fell upon her as Zeus had once fallen upon Danae. I remembered kissing the smooth concavity of her navel, and (oh Lord) dragging my tongue lower and lower until it dipped into the coppery canyon between her thighs.

'Penny for your thoughts,' says Angelika Ikon, as I stand beside her like a petrified sommelier.

Returning to the present I pour the ruby wine.

'*L'chayim*,' says Angelika Ikon, raising her glass.

Far below us little boats with unknown crews leave their temporary mark on the ultramarine tide.

Now Angelika Ikon is in the kitchen, wearing the apron formerly favoured by my wife. I watch as she fills a large pot with water and splashes some extra virgin olive oil into a skillet. She boils linguine in the former, and sautés sausages in the latter, slicing them as they spit snake-like under the blade. Finally she adds garlic, pepper, and the curly arugula, which quickly wilts in the pan. Within minutes she has a plate of food in either hand. She eats enthusiastically, twisting her fork as if her plate were a clock that needed constant rewinding.

'Here's an astonishing fact,' she says, as we complete the meal. 'In all the years we have worked together, I never once set eyes upon your better half. If you can bear it (and I wouldn't blame you if you couldn't), I'd love to see a portrait of the poor woman.'

Oh, I can bear it, and so can my wife.

Like some Barbary Coast barker, I summon my guest to the peep show, not with a raised voice, but by patting the vacant cushion on the settee beside me.

'A view from the kitchen window,' I say, holding aloft a 10×8 of my wife, bare-breasted and splayed like a spatchcock. I select half a dozen others from the portfolio.

'This is my wife posing in the bath *à la* Marthe

Bonnard,' I say, 'and this is her sunbathing in the style of Eve. And here's one I snatched when she was resting on the floor at the conclusion of her yoga exercises (which she performed upon rising, invariably in the buff).' Why am I doing this? Have I taken leave of my senses? I blame the potent wine, which must have unseated my reason. Angelika Ikon reviews the exhibition in silence.

'Mazel tov,' she says at length. 'Your missus undoubtedly possessed the finest breasts west of the Mississippi. Even so, don't you think there's something odd about all these prints?'

'Odd?' I enquire.

'I asked to see a likeness of your wife,' she replies, 'and yet her face is not visible in any of them. Isn't that odd?'

She's right! Nearly every post-Andersen portrait is cropped at the neck. You can see my wife's breasts or pudenda often enough, but never her head. She is always headless. Always faceless.

'I'm not saying you're Henry the Eighth,' Angelika Ikon continues, 'but you do seem to have a disquieting taste for decapitation.'

'I'm too squeamish to cut the head off a rose,' I protest, 'let alone the woman I loved.'

'You loved her body, for sure,' she replies, 'but did you love her mind as well? Perhaps you felt threatened by her determination to think for herself, and took revenge the only way you knew how. Why else would you show off this domestic pornography, except to humiliate her? No, I do not doubt your claim to have loved your wife, my friend, but I also believe that in some dark part of your heart you wished her ill.'

'That's a vile slander,' I say.

'Either way,' she replies, 'I now know why you're such a big fan of Les Krims. Make no mistake, it isn't your wife you have exposed to public scrutiny, but your own perverted soul.'

'Some comforter you've turned out to be,' I complain. 'In your self-righteousness you seem to have forgotten the possibility that I might find reviewing the photographs painful. As it happens, I do. I feel pain seeing what I once had and have now lost.'

The espresso machine in the kitchen lets off steam on my behalf, and I exit to collect the coffee. Returning with two cups and a plate of cookies on a tray, I find Angelika Ikon making eyes at my wife's doppelgänger on the wall.

'I'm sorry if I was a touch insensitive,' she says. 'It's simply that I find it impossible to remain neutral on the subject of female nudity.' She points to the framed photograph she has been studying. 'At least with this one I can talk about the face. Is it a good likeness?' she asks.

'It's an excellent likeness,' I reply, 'considering that it isn't my wife. Have some coffee, and I'll explain.'

'It's a funny thing,' says Angelika Ikon, when I have finished, 'but those eyes, that figure, that pose, all remind me of someone or something, but I'll be damned if I can remember who or what.' Only after Angelika Ikon has left do I recognize an echo of the words John Wayne had spoken within earshot of my wife.

Spring passes and summer succumbs to fall before I hear from Angelika Ikon again. She calls with a request to meet at Tobaccus. 'It's the perfect place to present the little proposition I have for you,' is as far as she will go. The appointed day is warm and the café's windows are all open, admitting a refreshing breeze and the nautical sound of seals barking. Angelika Ikon is awaiting me at a table for two.

'Remember that ill-tempered minx who served us last time?' she asks.

Having taken my seat, I nod.

'Well,' she continues, 'it's like Rita Hayworth in Schwab's Drugstore all over again. A producer comes in for a latte and Danish. Spots the miserable wench and immediately offers her a part in his next movie. Can you believe it? I ask Dio (the guy who runs this place), "Did that cheer her up?" Apparently not. Seems you can only expect one miracle per diem. Even here.'

I order a glass of Zinfandel from a Veronica Lake lookalike, who wiggles her behind on the off-chance.

Angelika Ikon sips her café au lait and licks off the
consequent moustache.

'Okay,' she says, 'here's the pitch. It seems that the
only camera obscura left in the city is under threat
of closure. If you've visited it you'll know that it's a
real eye-catcher, a building whose form describes its
function. California used to be full of such visual jokes
and come-ons. Alas, not many remain. So far we've
tracked down a large shoe in Bakersfield, within which
you can get your own repaired; a dinosaur outside an
oversized diner in Cabazon; a donut serving the same
in Ingelwood; and a chili bowl in west L.A. run by a
man who squares up to the multiples, and – you'll
like this – styles himself the Lone Ranger. I've also
heard of a bulldozer in Turlock, housing a company
that manufactures them. Nearer home there's a giant
artichoke in Castroville.'

'I know the place well,' I say. 'When returning from
a day at Point Lobos or Moss Landing, I frequently
make a detour to sample their world-famous French-
fried artichoke hearts, not to mention their equally
celebrated artichoke pie. I like the idea of eating a
vegetable within the confines of a greater one.'

'I'm glad that you share my enthusiasm for the
subject,' says Angelika Ikon. 'I just hope you share it
sufficiently to want to record the survivors. I'm well
aware that you prefer to work with animate objects,

but I'm confident that you'll make an exception for me, if not for them.'

It may be my imagination, but I'd swear that Angelika Ikon is acting coquettishly.

'Well,' she whispers, 'is my confidence misplaced?'

'To tell you the truth, I'd do it for anyone,' I reply. 'Such assignments were bread and butter to my father. If they were good enough for him, they're certainly good enough for me.'

'Now that's settled,' says Angelika Ikon, 'I have some news that might interest you. It concerns the photograph of the woman I mistook for your wife. Do you recall that I said it rang a bell? For several days afterwards I tried to place it. Then, of course, other things intervened and it slipped my mind. In fact I didn't give it another thought until a couple of weeks ago, when I took a new lover. He's that rare thing: a feminist male who is neither impotent nor gay. After we had exchanged bodily fluids in a manner pleasing to both, we stayed up until the small hours swapping previous mistakes. One of the more minor on my part was a one-night stand with a member of Vanilla Fudge. The consequences were minimal. I didn't get pregnant, nor did I catch a sexually transmitted disease, but I did get a few of their albums for my sins. My new lover insisted that I play a couple of tracks by way of penance. Slipping the records from their sleeves, I found some forgotten billets-doux from the priapic guitarist preserved like wild flowers between the pages of an old book. To be honest, they weren't exactly love letters, but actually handwritten postscripts on otherwise impersonal mailings to members of the fan club. One, in particular, suddenly chimed loud and clear.'

So saying, Angelika Ikon removes two folded sheets of American quarto from her purse and flattens them on the table. A mind-expanding mix of poetry and psychedelic art is revealed. ' "Where we are going / and where we have been / error's showing," ' I read. ' "Let us begin / Hi-ho Silver – Away." Shouldn't it be Hi-yo Silver?'

'Ignore the verses,' she advises. 'Look straight into the crystal ball.'

I obey, and instantly experience the same shock I felt, all those years ago, when I saw my wife caught by the camera obscura. Angelic wings had been appended to the young woman within the ball, but otherwise she was the spitting image of the anonymous beauty on my wall.

'Of course I didn't turn pale as you have just done,' says Angelika Ikon, 'but I was excited all the same. So excited that I called up my old flame as soon as the new one had departed for work. Naturally he had no recollection of our fling, nor did he have any idea as to the young woman's identity. However, he did know the name of the artist. A man who – it so happened –

owed me a favour. Did he know who she was? You bet!'

Angelika Ikon pauses, to heighten my surprise.

'Allow me to introduce your wife's double,' she says, 'known briefly as Tombstone's Helen of Troy. Why? Because she was first engaged to the sheriff, then ran off with his deputy, thereby precipitating the infamous gunfight at the OK Corral. Have I said enough?'

'Are you telling me that I've got a photograph of Wyatt Earp's scarlet woman in my dining room?' I exclaim.

'More like his wife,' replies Angelika Ikon.

If my own wife were to regain her human shape, walk down from the mountain top, and enter the café, I don't think I could be more astounded. In some way – as yet unknown – a connection has been forged with the great lawman. This link, however tenuous, is of even greater value to me than my encounter with the Lone Ranger. The latter had certainly been my first hero, but when I grew older and cast off childish things, I looked for someone with a little more gravitas, someone who was grounded in reality. I found him when ABC began showing *The Life and Legend of Wyatt Earp*. To this day I can recite every word of its signature tune: 'Wyatt Earp, Wyatt Earp / Brave, courageous and bold. / Long live his fame, and long live his glory, / And long may his story be told.' I liked the sentiment, that a tale well told could trump death. Still do. Though I don't recall a Mrs Earp being part of the show.

My father never felt his position threatened by this new obsession. On the contrary, he encouraged it, furnishing me with a long black tux from his wardrobe, and purchasing the essential pistol and holster. He even got us tickets to see the show's star, Hugh O'Brian, in some long-forgotten theatrical extravaganza. All I remember is his grand entrance on a golden steed, a palomino. Unfortunately I didn't get to witness his exit, though I waited by the stage door for more than an hour, pacing the sidewalk, not in expectation of seeing Hugh O'Brian, whose personality was of no interest to me, but of saluting the man he impersonated to perfection. However, my patience was eventually rewarded: I did get to meet my hero's representative on earth, in strangely appropriate circumstances.

In the tenth grade, an Incredible Hulk type joined our class. He had a mean temper and fists to match. He liked to play poker in vacant classrooms until the timetable inconvenienced him.

One day I was walking down the corridor when I heard his voice, as evil as ever: 'If Hitler really gassed six million kikes, how come there are so many of you in this neck of the woods?' As I got closer, I heard him yell: 'Fight, you damned Yids! Fight, you cowardly

sons of bitches!' Then there was silence, punctuated
only by his crazy laughter.

God knows why, but I entered the classroom. The
ape was surrounded by a quartet of reluctant pugilists.

'You fellows get back!' I shouted, with unexpected
authority. 'Move!' Finally I faced their tormentor.
'Come on, Hulk,' I said, 'we'll go over to the calaboose.'

I don't suppose it was the realization that we were
faithfully re-enacting an episode from Wyatt Earp's
early life that stayed his hand. A more likely cause
of his momentary paralysis was astonishment, occa-
sioned by the fact that a wimp had dared to call his
bluff. Anyway, in the split second he allowed before
launching the punch that would break my jaw, I
pinned him to the wall with an upturned chair. Of
course he would have brushed it aside in a matter of
seconds if a passing teacher hadn't intervened.

'I don't know your name,' he said to me, 'but
whoever you are, you've just earned yourself a ticket
to the HOBY Leadership Seminar.'

I could hardly believe my ears. HOBY was an
acronym. H stood for Hugh, OB for O'Brian, and Y for
Youth Foundation. The whole being a philanthropic
organization established after the actor had spent
nine inspirational days with the great humanitarian,
Albert Schweitzer, at his clinic in darkest Africa. Its
mission? To seek out, recognize and develop leadership
potential in high school sophomores to prepare the

next generation of civic and corporate leadership.
Every year educational establishments were invited to
send selected high-flyers to the aforementioned HOBY
Leadership Seminar where they would interact with
movers and shakers from big business, education,
government, and the professions, and thereby learn
about free enterprise and the American Way. I was one
of them? So it seemed. When confirmation came in
the mail I persuaded my parents to invest in a Junior
Wyatt Earp outfit, arguing that I would look poor and
foolish in my father's cast-offs.

I had recently taken unjustified criticism from one
teacher; now it was time to reap the harvest of unde-
served praise from another. Perhaps there was some
pattern to life after all, some system of checks and
balances, some divinely controlled distribution of just
desserts. Anyway, I had followed Wyatt Earp's prescription to the letter, as a result of which I was going
to meet his present-day incarnation.

Resplendent in new duds, I strode into the conference centre, only to be assailed with the certainty
that I had gatecrashed the wrong event: instead of
Earp clones, the auditorium was packed with miniature Republicans in short-sleeved white drip-drys or
Wall Street suits, and several dozen full-blown adults
dressed exactly the same. Instead of aged leather and
cordite, the characteristic perfume was Old Spice after-
shave. Who were these people? Then Hugh O'Brian

himself ascended the podium and I knew for sure that there was no mistake.

'Modern youth is in the public eye,' he began, 'because it steals cars, vandalizes schools, creates disturbances, and generally rebels against society. But I know and you know that these headline-makers represent only a small part of our teenage population. It is a fact that 98.7 per cent of our young people are law-abiding citizens. I think it's time we gave you good guys and good gals a pat on the back.'

This was not what I had come to hear. These were the words of Wyatt Earp's goody-goody twin. Who cared about the law-abiders? It was the outlaws – that other 1.3 per cent – who interested me and provided Earp and his ilk with their reputations. I looked again at the man on stage. His hair was as thick and as wavy as it appeared on the screen. His smile was just as winning. But in place of a shoestring tie he was sporting the colours of some country club. Nor was his suit sleek and dark. It was cut conventionally and had a white handkerchief protruding from the top pocket. And where, oh where was the fancy waistcoat and the black hat? Not to mention the Buntline Special.

'Will an individual be a taker or a giver in life?' O'Brian asked, by way of conclusion. 'Will that person be satisfied merely to exist, or seek a meaningful purpose? Will he or she dare to dream the impossible dream?'

For a terrible moment I thought he was going to burst into song, but what he had said was bad enough. I was there, not because I had dreamed the impossible dream, but because I had miraculously annexed a demigod's magical powers. Even as the others applauded I wept for my lost illusions. Oh, I knew as well as those who kowtowed to ersatz Emperor Norton that Hugh O'Brian wasn't really Wyatt Earp. But until then I had been happy to go along with the pretence that he was. This was no longer possible. Not because of O'Brian's right-wing politics. Nor even because of his copywriter's prose. It was simply the fact that, seen out-of-character, there was absolutely no trace of Wyatt Earp about him.

The HOBY Leadership Seminar was scheduled to last for three days. I didn't even make it through the first night. If only I had stuck it out. But how was I to know that in leaving prematurely I was depriving myself (and my father) of one of life's great moments? On the second day John Wayne unexpectedly showed up. Had I stayed I would have seen him put his great arms around Hugh O'Brian and would have heard him say: 'Hey, kid, you do a terrific Wyatt Earp. I knew him and you're terrific. I often think of Wyatt Earp when I play a film character. There's a guy who actually did what I'm trying to do.'

I continued to watch The Life and Legend of Wyatt Earp, but I was merely going through the motions.

I had lost my faith. I no longer believed in Hugh O'Brian. I could see the joins between character and actor. My father, hating to see me so crestfallen, quickly got to the source of my unhappiness. 'You must not blame God for the quality of his rabbis,' he said. 'If one rabbi disappoints, find another. But do not abandon God.' I grasped the analogy and sought a new leading man to act as my hero's surrogate. There was only one possible candidate. What did it matter that he had never actually played Earp in a movie? Like father, like son; I hitched my star to John Wayne.

Now I repeat those three words of his like a mantra – 'I knew him . . . I knew him' – and understand why my child-bride had looked so familiar to that household god of yore. If he had chewed the fat with Wyatt, he had almost certainly met Mrs Earp, and probably glimpsed the risqué portrait on display in the house, which was where he had seen the pubescent virgin before. I think of his failure to make the connection as symbolic. It was left to me to marry Wyatt Earp's girl.

Not that I subscribe to Doctor X's tomfoolery, will not believe for even a nanosecond that Mrs Earp's earthbound soul entered some vacant cavity within my nascent wife's body. However, her utterances while under his spell cannot be dismissed with such easy insouciance. They were clearly something other than babbling. And it was obviously more than coincidental that my wife not only owned a photograph of Mrs Earp, but also unconsciously assumed her persona. As far as I am able to see, there are three explanations (of diminishing probability). One: knowing the subject of the photograph was Mrs Earp, and tickled by the resemblance, my wife read what she could about the woman, and – under hypnosis – spilled out the other's life as her own. Two: Mrs Earp was more than my wife's accidental double, was in fact her ancestor, and a font of oral history. Three: that this ancestor's experiences were actually encoded in my wife's DNA, and could only be disclosed as recovered memories. But each possibility produced its own problems. If my wife had consulted books about the Earps, where were they? There were certainly none in the apartment. Furthermore, my wife was one hundred per cent Jewish, meaning that all her female ancestors would have had to have been Jewish too. Wyatt Earp's wife Jewish? Not very likely, I fear. But not impossible either; after all, she looked like my wife, who did look Jewish, in so far as her hair was dark and curly, and her complexion an impure white.

That impure white presence has begun to dominate my apartment. From a silent pin-up measuring 5×12 inches she has grown into an insistent apparition. Her transparent shift has become a shroud, clinging to a torso that is fading into the white background. Just as the definitive edges of my wife are beginning to soften.

Hoping to keep the latter in focus, I assiduously review the voluminous archive dedicated to her body. To no avail.

Perhaps because 'focus' is not *le mot juste*, there being more to my wife than met the eye. I need to do something other than look; I must map her interior, mark down the topography of her soul, fill in those regions still marked *pays inconnu*. Some features, such as Mount Andersen, might have been better left unexplored, but Lake Earp is too tempting to ignore. Besides, I have hopes that its hidden depths will not only hold information about the life and times of the mysterious Mrs Earp, but also reveal some untold truths about my wife. To prepare for this voyage of discovery, I march down Grant to Columbus, enter City Lights Bookstore and purchase every available volume on the subject of the Earps. Returning with my booty I put away my cameras and pick up my specs. As I begin to peruse the first book, the frame on the wall splits from side to side and Mrs Earp steps forth in all her youthful pulchritude.

All I knew about her was that she had met Wyatt Earp in Tombstone. By then she was – I soon discovered – a long way from home. Born in Brooklyn, but raised in San Francisco, she was a giddy, stage-struck girl with no equipment but her looks. Eventually they got her into trouble, but before that they got her into a company of thespians about to embark

on a tour of the Wild West, with (of all things) a
production of *HMS Pinafore*. Even more unexpected
than the frontier's enthusiasm for Gilbert and Sullivan
was the question the future Mrs Earp asked herself on
first setting foot in Arizona territory: What's a nice
Jewish girl doing in a place like this?

Needless to say, her parents – Hyman and Sophie
Marcus, formerly of Germany – knew nothing about
this little adventure. Without telling them, their school-
age daughter – Josephine or Josie – had boarded a
steamer bound for Santa Barbara, where the perform-
ances were scheduled to begin. From there the actors
travelled west, usually in two stagecoaches. As they
commenced the last leg of their journey they were
warned that a band of Apaches had jumped the reser-
vation and were on the warpath. By the second day
smoke signals were a common sight. As ever, there
was no smoke without fire. The Apaches appeared in
the late afternoon and started to spook the stage. The
driver whipped the horses to a gallop, but the hostiles
maintained the same distance between themselves and
their intended victims. Josephine had already given
herself up for lost when another group of riders suddenly sprang from the arroyo and put the Apaches to
flight. The skittish travellers were advised by their
saviours to take refuge in a nearby ranch, which they
did for ten days. One of the bold cavaliers happened
to be the sheriff of Tombstone, a charmer with merry

black eyes; Johnny Behan by name. Anyway, he charmed the pants off our heroine, who subsequently blamed her pathetic resistance upon the romantic circumstances. The handsome couple set up house together in Tombstone, until Josie caught her fiancé questioning a female suspect without his clothes. How she supported herself thereafter is unknown; her detractors maintain that she became a prostitute, though they provide no evidence other than the size of her breasts.

Hearing that Josie and Behan had parted, Wyatt decided to try his luck. She had the finest tits in Tombstone, he sported the grandest moustaches; it was a match made in heaven. Behan regarded this new liaison as a bad omen; having stolen his girl, Earp was bound to go after his job. Thus an otherwise insignificant affair initiated a feud that ended in bloodshed and made the final battleground as famous as Troy.

The climax occurred on an unseasonably windy afternoon in October 1881. Warned that trouble was brewing, Wyatt, Morgan, and Virgil Earp, accompanied by driller-killer Doc Holliday, decided to take a walk along Fremont. At the far end of the street they could see Behan in conference with his cronies, the Clantons, and the McLaurys. One of the Earps shouted, 'We have come to disarm you.' Behan shouted back: 'I have disarmed them.' It was a lie. Afterwards he insisted that Wyatt and his brothers had shot down unarmed men as if they were dogs. Another lie.

What really happened was that Billy Clanton fired off a pistol at Wyatt, who chose to plug Frank McLaury instead, knowing that he was the better shot.

'You sons of bitches have been looking for a fight,' shouted the most famous of the Earps, 'and now you can have it!'

After that all hell broke loose. Tom McLaury pointed his gun at Doc Holliday and sneered: 'I've got you now.'

'You're a daisy if you do,' quipped Holliday, before blasting his antagonist to kingdom come with both barrels of his shotgun.

Though fatally wounded, Frank McLaury managed to wing both Morgan and Virgil before being finished off with a bullet just below the right ear. Such were the noises my wife apparently heard when mesmerized by Doctor X. She also delivered an extremely accurate description of Josie's frenzied dash from her house to the killing ground, a vacant lot between the OK Corral and the boarding house where Doc Holliday lodged with his mistress, Big Nose Kate.

Holliday's landlord, Camillus S. Fly, was also the proprietor of Tombstone's only photographic studio and gallery. It was no mere sideline. In fact Fly was responsible for two of the most famous images to come out of the Old West: the shot of Billy Clanton and the

McLaury brothers, upright in their Sunday best and their coffins, *en route* to Boot Hill; and the last iconic portrait of Geronimo as a free man. It was in Fly's studio (or so it is assumed) that Josie slipped out of her street clothes and posed for her audacious carte de visite. If so it must have been taken about the time his backyard was used as a shooting gallery by her past and present beaux. In which case why was my copy stamped 'Kaloma' and dated 1914?

•

I ask Angelika Ikon to enquire whether the hippie responsible for the Vanilla Fudge artwork had ever set eyes on Fly's original. He hadn't. His source had been a flyer for a play called 'Quiet, Wyatt'. I contact the dramatist. She can do no more than refer me to the jacket of *I Married Wyatt Earp*, a book I have already read from cover to cover. Then Angelika Ikon calls with the news that she has spotted an exact replica of my photograph in a catalogue put out by Swann Galleries of New York. Further investigation turns up a second in a catalogue issued by Butterfield & Butterfield, auctioneers of San Francisco. Yet another is discovered in a catalogue from Balrog's Cards and Collectibles. The reserve on all three is in the region of $2500. 'Little is known about this image, beyond the identity of the sitter,' concludes one of my correspondents (Angelika Ikon's spiritual sister). 'But what is readily transparent is why it appeals to so many people.' What does she know, other than the market value of my heirloom? Neither she nor any of her fellow auctioneers can enlighten me as to the meaning of 'Kaloma', or explain why a photograph taken in the 1880s should be copyright 1914.

Gradually the word 'Kaloma' becomes my passport to insomnia. As it echoes through my sleepless nights I begin to think of it as a metaphysical concept; there's your 'Karma', and there's your 'Kaloma', the latter being the part of you that is forever unknowable to other people, and probably yourself too. Your *pays inconnu*. While others sleep, I orbit the dark side of my wife. And learn nothing. My only souvenirs are bags under the eyes.

Unfortunately it soon becomes obvious that it isn't only the meaning of 'Kaloma' that is obscure. Everything is uncertain, not excepting the identity of the person in the photograph (only the auction houses seem convinced that it is unquestionably Josephine Marcus Earp). Other authorities are more likely to call the identification 'disputed', or even 'bogus'. In fact this dispute is but a sideshow to a vendetta among Earp enthusiasts and scholars, a vendetta that is every bit as vicious as the bloody confrontation between the Earps and the Clantons. The quarrel over the photo's authenticity may only be a sideshow, but it is also a Rorschach test of sorts: what you see determines whether you are a cavalier or a roundhead, a romantic or a pedant, a believer or a doubter, a redskin or a paleface, a real man or a queer.

On the one side stands Glenn G. Boyer – author or editor of *I Married Wyatt Earp*; on the other is just about everybody else. Boyer's critics portray him as a historian manqué, a hoaxer, and a mischief-maker. They accuse him of fabricating history to make it more exciting and glamorous, in particular Josie Earp's memoirs (as well as her likeness). This is an ironic charge, given that Boyer made his name by debunking Stuart Lake, author of *Wyatt Earp: Frontier Marshall*, the book that first romanticized Earp's life and turned him into the stuff of legend, a man fit to be played by Burt Lancaster and Henry Fonda (not to mention Hugh O'Brian). Boyer promised to replace myth with the unvarnished truth. Now he is accused of applying an equal amount of varnish.

Boyer, for his part, sees himself as a living link to the most famous lawman of them all, John Wayne with pen and ink. In keeping with this image he lives on a ranch in a valley between the Chiricahua Mountains and the Peloncillos. Close by is the spot where Geronimo surrendered to the 4th Cavalry. Boyer is unlikely to follow his example. From his isolated hacienda he rails at his enemies, calling some homosexuals (especially if they make their home in San Francisco), and the rest mouthy bastards and chickenshit pricks.

This unmanly crew puts its faith in documentary
evidence, whereas Boyer rides the range in search of
witnesses and anecdotes. It was in Denver that he
heard a new version of the infamous gunfight, supposedly originated by Doc Holliday himself. He heard it
from a woman, who had heard it from her husband,
who had heard it from his father, a gambler, who used
to hang out with the Doc.

'I don't have it in writing,' Boyer continues. 'She
didn't have it in writing from her husband. He didn't
have it in writing from his father, who didn't have it
in writing from Doc Holliday.' Finally he asks: 'Do you
want this stuff brought down to you, or do you want
me to leave it to die somewhere?' It is a passionate
and convincing defence of oral history. So what if
the historian can't offer notarized and authenticated
documents to back up every claim? Why should words
on the page carry more weight – be more truthful –
than those that come straight from the tongue?

The trouble is that Boyer is also a self-confessed
prankster, a lover of practical jokes, making it virtually
impossible to separate fact from fiction. There's no
reason to doubt that he lived in Yuma in '56 or '57.
But did he really patronize a cantina run by a señorita
called Carmelita (he isn't sure, but thinks she was the
widow of a miner called Mayhew)? Although nearly
ninety, this Katy Jurado-type dyed her hair black and
wore it loose down to her waist as though she were

still the ravishing beauty she had once been. Boyer
treated her as such, and was rewarded with the info
that she knew 'where every body in Arizona is buried'.
She also knew Wyatt Earp and had been bosom
buddies with Josie. To prove the point she showed
Boyer the now famous photo of the said bosoms. 'How
come she posed like that in those days?' he asked. The
answer was simple: because Johnny Behan had got
her 'bombed on wine'. Even if that much is true, it
still leaves the problem of 'Kaloma', and the copyright
date of 1914.

Boyer has nothing to add on the subject of 'Kaloma'.
However, he is more inventive when it comes to the
anomalous date. He suggests that the original could
have been removed from Behan's effects after his death
in 1912 and thereafter exploited commercially. But
he also offers a more colourful explanation: what if
Behan, in his cups, sold the photograph to support his
alcoholism, and (as a bonus) got even with his old
rival by showing Mrs Earp's lovely tits to the world?
Boyer's conclusion is short and sweet: 'If it isn't Josie,
it ought to be.'

Unfortunately things are too often not what they
ought to be. And if the woman in the photograph isn't
who she ought to be, who is she? And does it mean
that my wife was kidding herself when she identified
so closely with the woman it isn't? If it isn't Josie, that
is, which is by no means proven. What if I willingly

suspend my disbelief? What if I give Boyer the benefit of the doubt and accept that the woman in the photograph is exactly who he says she is? What if I choose to believe that I was married to Wyatt Earp's great-granddaughter? What harm will I be doing? Of course I cannot produce any birth certificates, but I am not short of evidence either.

I had often wondered why my wife had insisted upon retaining her maiden name despite it being such an uncomfortable fit. 'It was the only thing my grandmother inherited from the parents she never knew,' she had explained. 'She hung on to it, even after marriage. As did my mother. As will I.'

Only now do I understand its significance. Perera is Spanish of course; it means a pear orchard or a cultivator of pears. Nothing extraordinary in that, save for one vital detail. Pear is an anagram of Earp. Real Pereras were often marrano Jews, Jews who retained a distant memory of their beginnings. My wife seems to have been a marrano Earp. It is worth noting that the caption under Josie's portrait in the Swann Galleries catalogue confidently states that she and Wyatt had three children together, a fact hitherto successfully hushed up by all other researchers and biographers. If this is accurate, one of the offspring was indubitably my wife's grandmother. She and her siblings were probably conceived sometime between 1893 and 1896, when the Earps were temporary residents of our city, in any one of three establishments: the residence on McAllister (where the itinerants lived with Josie's sister), the house on Ellis (the most likely location, where the Earps dwelt briefly in connubial bliss), or the apartment on 7th Avenue (where Wyatt stabled the horses that sustained his yen for gambling). The couple's peripatetic lifestyle obviously did not permit them to raise children. Accordingly they had each of their accidental progeny adopted. But they didn't want them entirely ignorant of their ancestry: they left them all a clue, the surname Perera. It is Angelika Ikon who adds the final touch, observing that 'Kaloma' is an anagram of 'OK Alma'.

Alma Perera equals Kaloma Earp. QED.

If I had only been more like Wyatt Earp than Johnny Behan. Then I certainly would not have behaved like a yellow-bellied coward (the type who shows dirty snaps of his wife by way of revenge), and would have faced up to Andersen man to man – like Wyatt would have done – and flushed him out of my system once and for all. But unlike my wife I am not descended from heroes. I am my father's son, and it is my destiny to load cameras, not guns, to shoot film, not bullets. Hence the familiar journey to Angelika Ikon's office to discuss the details of my next assignment: the photo-essay on buildings in fancy dress. As it turns out, Angelika Ikon is far more interested in the continuing story of the Earps.

'Tell me what happened after Tombstone,' she demands.

'How come you're suddenly so interested?' I ask. 'Isn't Josie Earp exactly the sort of woman a woman like you despises? You're a feminist. She was a gun-slinger's floozy, and a pin-up. What could the pair of you possibly have in common?'

'*Pays inconnu*,' she replies. 'A love of lighting out for unknown territory. She was a pioneer, a foremother, and therefore worthy of respect.'

'You are right about the call of the wild,' I say. 'Like a thousand others the Earps went to Alaska in search of gold, but only really hit pay-dirt when they drifted back to Hollywood. Once settled, Wyatt took to visiting the studios. Actors were flattered by his attention; felt they were in contact with authenticity. Strolling around the backlots with a sidekick (Jack London, no less), he bumped into Charlie Chaplin. Chaplin, it seems, had heard of Earp: "You're the bloke from Arizona, aren't you? Tamed the baddies, huh?" He hung around with the likes of William S. Hart, John Ford, and a beefy extra still known as Marion Morrison. And then he died.'

'Is that the end of the story?' asks Angelika Ikon.

'No,' I reply. 'Like all stories his ends in a graveyard.'

'Which one?' she asks.

'A local one,' I say. 'The Hills of Eternity Memorial Park.'

'It's too good to be true!' exclaims Angelika Ikon.

'That's what I thought,' I reply, 'but there's no mistake. Wyatt Earp, the Hercules who cleaned the Augean stables of Tombstone, lies beside his wife in a Jewish cemetery.'

'We must write finis to their tale,' says Angelika Ikon. 'We must visit their graves immediately.'

We speed along El Camino Real in Angelika Ikon's silver soft-top (a rare Hermes), while the evening fog rolls down the western hills like cream poured over Black Forest gateau. At the cemetery they provide us with a map which highlights the path to Wyatt Earp's final resting place. We drive slowly along the main drag until we reach the sixth sidewalk, at which point there is a mausoleum large enough to accommodate one of the ten tribes. From there we continue on foot, turning right and properly entering the dwelling of the multitude, a petrified forest, where stone stumps grow out of old bones. Each stump has a name – Adler, Weiss, Zelinsky – but no story. Only the Earps can boast of that, whole histories being compressed in that famous surname. I try to picture the glorious couple as they really were, but even in this solemn place all I can see is Josephine in her transparent shift, and John Wayne walking the walk. Is it such a bad thing? Is it such a bad guise in which to spend eternity? The dead are the last people who need be troubled by reality. We place two pebbles on the grave to mark our visit. Previous pilgrims have left cards (the ace of hearts), and gambling chips. Inscribed upon the black marble is the inscription: ' . . . That nothing's so sacred as honor, and nothing so loyal as love!'

As I make a detour in order to pay my respects to my parents and my uncle with the head for heights, Angelika Ikon suddenly pauses at a newer stone.

'Alma Perera,' she reads. 'Isn't that your wife's name? You didn't tell me she is buried here.'

'She isn't,' I reply, 'it's just a coincidence.'

If only. Try as I might I cannot deny the memory that comes unbidden, the memory of my wife on her deathbed in the cancer ward. She was naked beneath a sheet that kept slipping off to reveal a skeletal body with a fleshless dug and skin as wrinkled as bark. The only thing that continued to look healthy was the silicone prosthetic. Nor can I shut out the sound effects: remembered shrieks of agony echoing in my head like hideous birdsong. Why could no one quieten her? Where was Dr Kildare when he was really needed? Not that he could have done any good. She was beyond the skill of doctors. Her disease had outsmarted them all. It tortured her at will. Her sole relief was a mechanical pump, which issued doses of morphine to deaden both pain and mind. If only she had turned into a Bristlecone Pine, or even run off with Andersen. Anything rather than what really happened . . .

Angelika Ikon is saying something, but all I can hear are Alma's last coherent words: 'They cannot let me die,' she cried. And then, finally: 'How can I die? I am too rooted in life to die.'

I have tried – God knows – to prove her right. But in the end only God can quicken the dead.

iii

As her grip on terra firma grew weaker, my wife was festooned with transparent tubes. Nourishment flowed freely through them, as through the aerial roots of a febrile house plant. To no avail. Nothing, it seemed, could salvage her vitality. She withered before my very eyes.

'Please be frank,' I said to Surgeon B. 'Are you still confident that my wife can be cured?'

His colleague, a young intern, turned green.

'Her lungs are still clear,' replied Surgeon B. 'That is always a good sign.'

'But it isn't an answer to my question,' I said.

Surgeon B looked straight at me. 'You want my honest opinion?' he snapped. 'Very well. In my opinion, your wife is dying. She has three weeks left. Four at the most.'

I did not flinch, though the words took my breath away as effectively as a blow to the solar plexus. I remembered Surgeon B's initial prognosis: that my wife would almost certainly live out her biblical span. I did not call him a liar, or even remind him of his false prediction. He had been guided by statistics, and statistically my wife should still be alive, should still be living flesh and bone, not cold ashes under a stone. But that is where she is, lying within sight of Wyatt and Josephine Earp (who may or may not have been her great-grandparents). Although I am a non-believer, I recite the Kaddish. Seeing me at prayer, Angelika Ikon obviously realizes that I am fibbing about my wife's posthumous whereabouts, but for once keeps a tactful silence. At least until we begin our return journey in her sporty argentine roadster.

'What was that mumbo-jumbo you were uttering over the mortal remains of the woman who wasn't your wife?' she asks, as we join the flow of traffic heading for the city.

'A prayer for the dead that doesn't mention death,' I reply.

'So what's the point of it?' she asks, switching lanes to pass a truck with Tennessee plates.

'To praise the Almighty,' I reply. 'It begins: "May his great name be exalted, and sanctified throughout the world, which he hath created according to his will." '

'Typical,' says Angelika Ikon. 'Your God gives your wife terminal cancer, and you say "thank you". Why didn't you demand a few answers instead? Such as: "What had my wife ever done to you to merit such a cruel reward?"'

Angelika Ikon hits the gas pedal and contemptuously accelerates past a bone-white stretch-limo with inky windows.

'Of course such questions are unnecessary if you drop the foolish notion of divine justice,' she continues. 'I'm sure you're familiar with the infamous exchange that took place between two Nazis in occupied Poland. "I killed your Jew," boasted the first. "In that case, I'll kill yours," said the other. And he did. The probability is that the omnipotents who really do control our destinies behave in a like manner. Maybe your wife inadvertently offended one of the meaner gods, and her own protector was powerless to shield her. Surely that fits the facts better than the crackpot notion of a benign old patriarch with a long beard.' She laughs, and pats my thigh. 'I know I'm wasting my breath,' she says. 'You Jews are so fucking obstinate. You'll never abandon your God, even though all available evidence points to his non-existence. The only other possible interpretation is that he hates your guts.'

'If it's all the same to you,' I reply, 'I'll stick to not believing in one god, it's so much less effort than not believing in a score.'

We are inching our way up California Street, at the summit of which stands the newly constructed Temple of Diana with its dazzling alabaster columns and its polychromatic frieze illustrating some bucolic knees-up. The eponymous goddess is depicted as a pink-cheeked huntress, though her bow-string is slack, and her arrows all still in their quiver. She certainly strikes no fear in the quarry; deer frolic around her dainty feet as though she were actually Francis of Assisi.

'And what makes you so confident that the neo-classical pastiche out there is anything more than an empty gesture?' I ask. 'Where is the evidence that confirms the hegemony of Zeus and his fellow Olympians?'

'Evidence?' cries Angelika Ikon. 'Why, the whole world is a memorandum that they exist!'

Before I can offer an objection, Angelika Ikon bangs the horn and salutes some startled vestal virgins on the sidewalk. They are even more startled when hirsute faces stealthily emerge from behind the columns, like brigands springing an ambush in a forest. As they come leaping out into full view, their true identity is immediately apparent: not bandits, but Hasidim. Screaming insults ('Whore!', 'Pagan!') and flapping their black gabardines, they advance upon their adversaries like a flock of ravenous crows. The vestal virgins take one look at their outlandish foes, utter a squeal or two, then raise the hems of their long white shifts and flee for their lives (an unnecessary precaution, needless to say, since a religious Jew is allowed no

physical contact with any woman other than his wife).
It ain't exactly the gunfight at the OK Corral, but as
the triumphant Hebraists celebrate their victory over
the Hellenists, I note the wingspan of their moustaches, their black capotes, and their broad-brimmed
hats, and cannot help but think of the Earp brothers.
I have a pleasant daydream in which Wyatt patrols the
meaner streets of heaven, his deputy marshal's badge
replaced by a shining Star of David.

Next day I'm on the road again, alone in my own
Impala, *en route* to Castroville. Fierce storms have
been forecast and I'm anxious to use the lightning for
dramatic effect. To be honest I am hoping to emulate
a great photograph by Max Yavno, who was close to
my father on account of their similar backgrounds
and identical professions. My father, incidentally, was
never envious of his friend's greater fame; Yavno's
archive now resides in Arizona, but no university has
enquired after my father's, not while he was alive, nor
since his death. Anyway, Max Yavno took this fantastic
shot outside Sanderson's Hosiery on Olympic Boule-
vard. It is dark, the company's neon logo is aglow. A
couple of street lights shine. Otherwise all is black,
save for the astonishing central image. A woman's
shapely leg, a limb of gigantic proportions, has apparently emerged from the night sky and is touching a
drum-like plinth with its toes (which, of course, are
sheathed in one of Sanderson's stockings). Venus

stepping out of her bath couldn't be more striking or beautiful. Alas, Sanderson's Hosiery has long since been demolished. All that remains of it is Yavno's photograph. It's quite an epitaph.

Like my father, Yavno preferred to work in black and white. Wildlife photography generally does not allow such artistic licence. Because the natural world is colourful, and animals pattern themselves accordingly, I am compelled to use colour film; Kodachrome for preference. No artistry must be apparent in such images; on the contrary, they must seem to be an unmediated expression of the natural world. But the world I am about to photograph is anything but natural; it is witty, but also grotesque. A world populated by hypertrophied vegetables, shoes fit for Goliath, and donuts the size of Saturn's ring. And so, for the first time since the uncanny blizzard, the camera bouncing on the back seat of my auto is loaded with Tri-X. What luxury!

I reach Santa Cruz by sundown, and forty minutes later am setting up my tripod in the parking lot of the giant artichoke. The meteorologists have not misled me; the sky is black with a hint of plum. Lightning flickers on the tea-stained horizon, while plump raindrops burst upon the ground like overripe grapes. I miss the first flash of lightning. And the second. But I know the time between them. On the count of ten I open the shutter and wait. Not for long. Lightning suddenly rips through the night sky and strikes the Brobdingnagian artichoke which, in the ghastly light, looks like some mutant dreamed up by Dr Frankenstein. I remove my finger from the shutter. Max Yavno, eat your heart out!

•

With the giant artichoke in the bag, I decide to record our local treasures before checking out the bizarre fruits of the more abundant south. Last night's storm has freshened the air, and the light is scintillating over the north-west corner of the city. For once the Pacific is as good as its name. Even so, the former Playland-at-the-Beach is deserted, its roller coasters and carousels either shut down or moved elsewhere. Where children once squealed with terrified delight, feral mongrels now scuffle among drifting piles of orphaned garbage.

I am idly giving consideration to taking a few shots when my attention is distracted by a lone dog moving slowly across the concrete desert. Its mechanical gait makes it an obvious candidate for a hip replacement. The strays register it too, and divert their concentration from the slim pickings to the tottering creature; the humiliations have been too many, the temptation is too great. Seven or eight cast off their roles as scavengers and revert to the old ways, to the hunt. They form a pack and quickly surround the toothless hound. That done, the fiery-eyed fiends crouch and extend their necks. Their threatening growls sound like the rumble of an approaching juggernaut. The endangered dog ceases to move. It must know that its death resides in those sabre-toothed smiles, that those glistening pink tongues will shortly be awash with crimson. It is an extraordinary scene, and at another time I may well have let nature take its course and recorded the consequences. On this occasion, however, I decide to intercede, to try to save the old grey-beard. After all, these creatures are not killing out of necessity but out of simple viciousness; they are as bad as a band of self-loathing punks beating the living daylights out of a senior citizen. As I perform my quixotic gesture, I consider the possibility that they might forget about their intended victim and decide to do to me what their ancestors did to Actaeon. But I reckon that if I proceed with an unblinking stare, a fierce demeanour, and unthinking confidence the whelps will turn tail.

In fact they fail to register my approach, so engrossed are they in biting lumps out of the leaden-footed trespasser. Down it goes, leaving its neck unprotected and completely exposed. Two of the assassins immediately sink their foam-flecked teeth into its inviting throat.

At which point I arrive and kick the largest of the beasts in the ribcage. It grunts, turns, and hunches its shoulders, preparing to launch itself at me. As it begins to rise I swing my camera and bring it down to earth with a mighty blow. Using my new weapon as a sling I rout the remainder, scattering them in all directions. Their victim is silent and torn, but its chest still rises and falls. I kneel to read the dog tag hanging from its collar. On the obverse is the word 'Pluto', on the reverse is a representation of the camera obscura. 'Come, old friend,' I say, picking up the bloodied mutt, 'I'll take you home.'

It keeps its rheumy brown eyes fixed upon me as I ascend the concrete steps. I fancy that they are expressing something like gratitude. Its owner is somewhat more explicit. I could be wrong, but I'm sure his moustache was as white as his suit the last time we met. Either way, it's black today, as is his outfit.

'Good sir,' he says, taking possession of his pet (which weakly wags its tail), 'I am in your debt; in short, I owe you a life.'

'It was a mitzvah,' I reply. 'That is sufficient reward.'

'Not according to my code of honour,' replies the ageless keeper of the camera obscura. 'You saved my dog's life. Therefore I am duty-bound to offer you the same in exchange.'

'It's a lovely thought,' I say, 'but I don't think it would work. For one thing, I live in an apartment. For another, I'm always on the move.'

'Our good Samaritan has got the wrong end of the stick,' he says, addressing his dog. 'Perhaps he will grasp my meaning better if I reveal that you are not named after Mickey Mouse's co-star – as I always tell the kiddies – but after your immortal owner – ' he giggles – 'who has connections in low places.'

'Am I supposed to understand that I am in the presence of Pluto, King of the Underworld?' I ask.

'By Jove, your saviour is quick on the uptake,' he says, gently standing his dog on its own four feet.

I recollect the stories my father used to tell about our deluded ancestor, the self-styled Emperor Norton, and decide to humour him.

'If you really are the ruler of the infernal regions,' I ask, 'what are you doing in this obscure place?'

'A fair question,' he replies. 'As you know, we ancient deities have many names. In addition to Pluto, I am also known as Hades the Unseen, and (I am sorry to say) Orcus the Slayer. And we have as many different roles as we have names. As Pluto, one of my more pleasant responsibilities is bestowing the riches of the earth upon the worthy, which is what brought me to the far west in the first place. Everybody knew about the fabulous Comstock Lode, near Virginia City, Nevada, but no one knew how to get the ore out economically. To this end a shaft had been excavated to a depth of 1,500 feet, but great volumes of water continued to impede the progress of the miners. Pumping turned out to be costly and dangerous. Moreover, the temperature in the lower levels often exceeded 110 degrees Fahrenheit. Huge blocks of ice were hauled down to ease the lot of the toilers, but that act of charity was as laborious as the digging itself. As if those were not obstacles enough, the very air was so noisome that men who inhaled it for too long a time breathed their last in those poisoned caverns. These hindrances were noted by young Alfred Sutro, an immigrant formerly of Prussia, and (more lately) San Francisco. I visited him in a dream, and placed a single thought in his receptive mind: "Drain the mines."

'With daylight came the idea of constructing a four-mile-long tunnel beneath the workings. Hectoring and small-minded harpies mocked his ambition, derided him for believing that a gateway could be forced through granite. Where was the machinery? Where were his bonds and coined securities? It took fifteen years for his dream to become reality, but I made sure that his superhuman efforts did not go unrewarded. The hidden treasures of the earth surrendered them-selves to him in such abundance that he was dubbed the Comstock King. The body politic didn't do badly either. Indeed, I like to think that my nocturnal inter-vention led to the birth of modern America; after all, it was silver from the Comstock Lode that financed Lincoln's war to end slavery. As it happens, modern American literature was its twin. One of the rare pros-pectors not to thrive (I saw to that) was an eager miner from Missouri. After a few fruitless weeks he threw away his pick and decided to try his hand at writing, getting his first job as a reporter on the *Territorial Enterprise*. His name, as you must have guessed, was Samuel Clemens. Making me godfather to Tom Sawyer and Huckleberry Finn, as well as all their progeny. So, you see, it's not all gloom and doom being King of the Underworld; the job has its positive side.'

He bends down and affectionately strokes his canine namesake.

'What was it the gentleman asked me?' he mutters. 'Oh yes! Why am I here? Well, having made his fortune, Sutro abdicated while the going was good, then retired to this spot. I followed, out of curiosity, and have been a frequent visitor ever since. I feel at home here; the camera obscura is strangely reminiscent of my own substanceless empire. So much so that I have turned old Sutro's tunnel into one of my back doors. I suggest you make use of it before winter sets in. As I said, I owe you a life.'

'Are you telling me that all I need do to rescue my late wife from the Underworld is walk the length of the Sutro Tunnel, find her, and then return to the world of light?' I ask.

'You're right about one thing,' he replies. 'It's easy enough to gain admittance to my kingdom. The trick is to get out again. Not many manage that. To facilitate your safe return I'll give you a little pin to wear in your lapel which will act as a *laissez-passer*.'

At which point I feel compelled to explain to my would-be benefactor that the real purpose of my visit wasn't actually to save his dog's life but to take some pictures for an article on playful architecture for a magazine called *Pays Inconnu*.

'That's what you think,' he replies, before repairing to his kiosk in hopes of finding the promised tsatske.

While he is gone I finally prepare to photograph the exterior of the camera obscura (intending to make full use of the high-contrast light), only to find my viewfinder filled by the sight of an eccentric gent waving a jewel-like object.

'Another treasure from the Comstock Lode,' he explains, as he presses a tiny golden bough into my hand. 'The mine's silver enabled belligerence to prosper, but its gold (assuming you follow my directions) will effect a miraculous reconciliation. Whatever you do, don't lose it.'

The brooch is small but accurately formed, apparently fashioned after the holm oak. Its delicate gold leaves tickle my palm. There is no question: the bauble is astonishingly beautiful.

'See, Pluto has recovered from his ordeal already,' says Pluto's owner (and possible namesake), pointing to the sleeping dog. But he won't let mine lie. 'Has your wife been a resident of my dismal suburb for long?' he asks.

'About a year,' I reply.

'Accident or illness?' he asks.

'Illness,' I reply.

'Do you miss her?' he asks.

'Yes,' I reply. 'I also miss the man who loved her. I am a different man without her. And if I am a different man, I must have had a different history. And if I had a different history, my wife would not have figured in it. And if she didn't figure in it, how do I know she actually existed? Those intimate photographs could be of a stranger, an anonymous model. I need to see her again. To prove that she did exist. To be the man I was.'

'Believe me, you will,' he replies.

'I wish I could. Believe you, I mean.'

'I wish you could too,' he replies. 'Perhaps my familiars will succeed where my words have failed.'

So saying, he holds his cupped hands to his mouth and begins to produce the most extraordinary sounds: a long melancholy wail, rising from deep within his abdomen, alternates with a mix of clicks and thrums. Simultaneously the glassy water between the shore and Seal Rocks vibrates then shatters as a pod of orcas breaks surface. 'It's not proof conclusive,' he says, 'but it's certainly evidence.'

The black and white backs of the killers gleam in the sun.

'Why don't you take some pictures, while I go and

fetch a map,' says the man who has half convinced me that he really is a classical deity.

Why not? I have the appropriate film already loaded. I sprint to the edge of the escarpment, attach a tele-photo lens, and record some astounding seascapes with whales (the mishmash of light and water echoing their chiaroscuro hides).

'Be sure to take your Olympus with you,' says the pretender to Pluto's throne as he returns with the chart. 'The dead love to be photographed. Savages believe that cameras steal their souls. The dead are convinced the opposite is true.'

The map is not something you buy for a few cents at a gas station. It looks the part, being antique and hand-tinted. Not only does it reproduce the topograph-ical features in a conventional manner, it also displays elevations, and even includes an artistic representation of the mountains. The legend, printed in a lozenge, declares: 'Map Showing Exact Locations & Dimensions of the Sutro Tunnel & the Comstock Lode.'

'These days,' says my time-honoured guide, 'the tunnel's entrance is signposted by a State of Nevada Historical Marker (number 85 to be precise), which is located on Highway 50, approximately three miles east of Dayton. Dayton is marked on the map, as is Virginia City, Silver City, Gold Hill, as well as Sutro itself (now a ghost town). All the mines are shown too.'

He hands it to me. I politely demur.

'Take it,' he insists. 'You don't want to stumble down the wrong hole and get yourself permanently lost. The other important thing not to do is look back.'

The obvious way to get to Dayton, Nevada, from San Francisco is to take Highway 80 to Sacramento, and there join Highway 50, which (I have been assured) proceeds directly to Hades, just before Carson City Highway 50 crosses Highway 395, the road that took us through Lone Pine, Independence, and Bishop, *en route* to the Bristlecone Pines. It is a meeting of roads and of narratives. From now on the two stories will merge and be as one.

Speeding towards an alternative ending, I penetrate the land of quickie divorces and second marriages. The ubiquitous sun goes down behind my back, copperplating the modest city on the eastern horizon. Its name honours Kit Carson, first of the famous Indian fighters. He was also the first to be transformed into a fictional character for the titillation of easterners. A favourite subject of those pulpy texts was the abduction and debasement of white females by oversexed aborigines. The inspiration for this was not so much the murder of Jane McCrea, a real event, but more its hot-blooded representation in oils by Mr John Vanderlyn.

The doomed woman is on her knees. Above her are two naked savages; the first pulls back her hair, exposing her throat and her breasts (one of which is laid completely bare), while the second raises his tomahawk. 'Her kerchief torn betrays the globes of snow,' gloats a contemporary poet. 'That heave responsive to her weight of woe.' Angelika Ikon would be wise to the true subject of the painting: not murder, but rape. Thus women knew that, were they to be captured by hostiles, they would surely experience a fate worse than death.

There was just one hope. Hope was a man. Hope went by the name of Kit Carson. If he was on your trail you were as good as saved. At least that is what the dime novelists would have the world believe. In real life, of course, the endings were not always so happy. As Carson well knew. His biography, *The Nestor of the Rockies* (supposedly dictated by the unlettered old warrior himself), records the pursuit of a band of renegade Apaches who (true to character) had lately kidnapped a white woman. Alas, his surprise attack on the enemy camp did not result in the unhappy captive's salvation. Instead he found the poor woman with an arrow in her soft breast. Beside her still warm body was a dime novel, the cover of which showed Carson redeeming yet another damsel in distress. 'Oh George, we are saved!' cried the threatened heroine. 'The very presence of Kit Carson is safety.' The real Kit Carson felt shame for the false comfort this episode must have offered its most recent reader, now a rudely disillusioned corpse.

If the truth were told he didn't look much like his *alter ego* either. General William Sherman (who should have known better) was taken aback to meet 'a small stoop-shouldered man ... with nothing to indicate extraordinary courage or daring'. But such unprepossessing raw material didn't hinder the imagination of the dime novelists, nor should it have given the alchemists of Hollywood much pause for thought (using five-inch insteps they easily transformed a midget like Alan Ladd into a veritable giant). Kit Carson's actual achievements (even allowing for the occasional tragedy) were second to none. So how to explain his failure to graduate from dime-novel to Tinsel Town? There was a short-lived television series called *The Adventures of Kit Carson*, but it was *The Life and Legend of Wyatt Earp* that touched the national psyche. Everyone remembers Hugh O'Brian. But Bill Williams? Could crafty old Aristotle have the explanation for Carson's relative obscurity as an immortal? For one thing, his life had no unity of place, no equivalent of Tombstone. Nor did he participate in anything as cathartic as the gunfight at the OK Corral. When Aeneas visits the Underworld he is accosted by his deceased helmsman, Palinurus, who bellyaches about the raw deal he's getting from Pluto. He is only mollified when informed that a town will be named after him, thereby preserving his memory for ever.

I trust that being the capital of Nevada offers similar consolation to America's neglected hero.

By the time I'm on the far side of Carson City it is doubly dark; night has fallen, and with it has come the dreaded pogonip, a local phenomenon. The pogonip is a sort of anti-dragon which doesn't incinerate but freezes the surrounding fauna with its frosty breath. As I drive cautiously through swirling eddies of opaque air, my fog-lamps pinpoint numerous stands of glazed trees. They glitter like bejewelled silver birches (or their close relatives) and cause an inappropriate memory to stir. Jealousy, it would appear, has no doubts. I am able to suppress it (though not without mental strife) on the grounds that the trees are false prompts, being false birches.

It turns out that it could also be a false memory altogether. A couple of days after Surgeon B informed me that my wife's prospects were nil, she unexpectedly awoke from her delirium and said: 'I have a confession to make.'

'Not another infidelity,' I moaned. 'Not with Grimm too.'

'No,' she said, 'it's a confession about the confession.'

'There's more?' I said.

'On the contrary,' she said, 'there's less. Not a word of it was true. I never had a one-night stand, let alone an affair, with Andersen.'

'But if he didn't take the incriminating photograph, who did?' I said.

'Me,' said my wife, 'I did. Set the timer and jumped in the shower. It was a joke. I was going to give it to you when I got home, but you were such a grouch that I hid it instead.'

'But why didn't you tell me when I eventually did find it?' I asked increduously.

'You seemed so convinced of my infidelity that I felt it would be almost churlish to disappoint you,' she said, 'so I invented the story about Andersen. I was quite hurt to see how eagerly you swallowed it.'

So saying she subsided into her pillows and said nothing more until her death, save for the few words I have recorded elsewhere.

Deathbed confessions possess a gravitas it is hard to gainsay. Even so I wish I had thought to search for the negative – which of course would confirm my wife's second explanation – before I had emptied the apartment of her belongings. Without that I found it impossible to rid myself of nagging doubts. After all, her first story had been so convincing that the image of the adulterous pair copulating on the bosky greensward now lodged in my brain like a memory, false or otherwise. Even the truth – if that's what it was – couldn't flush it away.

After a while the trees thin out, and for a few minutes there is nothing but a foggy blank, until I

pass a pole that looks like an anorexic spruce and
realize that I have reached my destination: Nevada
historical marker number 85. I pull over, open the
door, and am immediately embraced by the icy exhalations of the pogonip.

My own breath is quickly absorbed by the greater
mass. I wonder if the afterlife will be like this, a vast
bank of freezing fog, each skein of which (and there
are billions) being another soul. I tread warily (for the
ground is rocky) towards the spectral remains of Sutro.
Its scattered buildings (now dimly visible) look as if
they were designed by infant architects: walls flat
and monochrome, windows square and symmetrical,
doors big and central. Being a ghost town there are
no inhabitants to point the way. I must find my own.
Fortunately I have a bespoke map to assist me. Now
comes the ingenious part. I am wearing a canary-
yellow hard hat with lamp attached (borrowed from a
generous speleologist). It quickly sheds light on the
problem of wither.

According to the map the tunnel is located at the
far end of the main street, where the town peters out
and the mountains begin. Its entrance is a gaping black
rectangle, tapering slightly in the manner of an Inca
doorway. Above it is an obtuse-angled roof, in shape
not unlike a coolie's hat. Putting incredulity on hold,
I cross the threshold and commence my descent. I
have come too far to permit scepticism to stop me now.

The outside world's weather penetrates for a few yards, whereupon the tunnel's microclimate imposes itself. It is cold and damp. And dark. I sample the air cautiously, remembering the tale of the deadly atmosphere, but there is no trace of methane, or carbon monoxide, or any other noxious gas; only the foetid whiff of stagnant water. Without was a melange of greys, within is uniform black. Or it would be if it weren't for my borrowed headpiece, which makes it look as if my own brainwaves are lighting the way. The walls are crudely cut and sometimes jagged. The sloping floor is the same. Not only is it uneven, it is also coated with a layer of sticky slate-coloured mud, which slows progress and makes slipping an ever-present possibility. By the time I have covered the four or five miles to the Tunnel's end, my backside has been battered black and blue. I say 'end', but it's actually a T-junction, with branches to left and right. I have been instructed to ignore both and proceed in a straight line. Through solid granite?

I examine the blind wall with greater care, and discover a small fissure just above head height. I gather sufficient debris to construct a platform. Standing upon it I am able to properly investigate the tributary. Having satisfied myself that it can easily accommodate a horizontal adult, I enter head first. Would I have done such a foolhardy thing if I couldn't already see the exit? Not that the exit is unproblematic. For all

I know it could tip me out into a bottomless pit. As it happens I am delivered like a newborn on to a wide ledge, unscathed but for a blue bib of mud. There is another significant detail worth noting. I am not alone.

There are hundreds – if not thousands – of people all drifting in the same direction: towards a bridge that connects the ledge to the continent. Though very few, it seems, are permitted to cross. To call these unwanted migrants black would be to mislead. 'Black' implies density, and these people have none. Their too too solid flesh seems to have thinned to such an extent that casting a shadow would be beyond their capabilities. On the contrary, the light would probably shine right through them. Not that there is any way of testing this impression. Although a dismal variant of daylight seems to be falling from the colourless and cloudless sky (or ceiling), there is no sun (nor any dark equivalent). And my own beacon has been extinguished, to avoid attracting undue attention.

Now that I am nearer the bridge I can see that it is an exact duplicate of Joseph Strauss's *coup d'éclat*, except that it isn't 'international orange' (like the original), but grey like everything else. You know what? It's just like looking at one of my father's black and white negatives blown up to life-size. Then it occurs to me that the people also resemble negatives. They are exactly like ambulant negatives, in need of light and chemicals to bring them fully to life. No wonder they are fascinated by the sight of my camera. Before long many are begging me to take their portraits and present the result to so and so, back in the old country. They give me messages to deliver, as if the living were all on first-name terms.

Eventually I actually see someone I recognize: a rival photographer who has oftentimes reached the scene of a rare sighting before me. The lucky bastard has beaten me to it again.

'What the hell are you doing here?' I demand. 'Planning to exploit these poor souls and clean up as a street photographer?'

'It so happens I am here by right,' he replies, 'which is more than I can say for you.'

Only then does it register that he is also a negative.

'Forgive me,' I say, 'it didn't occur to me that you were dead.'

'In a plane crash,' he replies, 'five days ago. The wreckage hasn't been located yet, so obviously I'm unburied. That's why I'm still on this side, among the paupers and the missing-feared-dead. Perhaps you could see to my cremation when you return. The plane went down in Antarctica, on the slopes of Mount Erebus. Shouldn't be too hard to spot.'

'I'll do my best,' I say.

'Please do,' he replies, 'otherwise I'll be stuck here for a hundred years, like these poor suckers.'

I push my way through the yielding multitude

until I come to the bridge's entry ramp. Before I can take another step, however, a hard-faced guardian with unkempt hair emerges from the tollbooth and says: 'What the fuck do you want? Don't you know the rule? No funeral, no entry. And you're not even dead. So beat it.'

'Perhaps this little keepsake from your boss will soften your attitude,' I reply, pointing to the golden bough gleaming upon my black lapel.

'Get back, the rest of you!' shouts the grim custodian. 'The positive can cross.'

Despite appearances, the bridge has sufficient substance to bear my weight. It's a long walk, and I have the leisure to wonder why I chose to recall the saddest episode of Kit Carson's eventful life. I analyse the images as if they had emerged from a dream. Of course! The arrow in the breast is the tumour that killed my wife. The dime novel represents the false prognosis. And Kit Carson is me, helpless in the face of malign fate. I wonder if my wife has any inkling that I am on the way. If so, is she doomed to disappointment or worse? I want to pray for success. But to whom? The gods of the Greeks and Romans? Or singular Jehovah? Either way, I plead that I will be given the strength to rescue my wife. Only then do I begin to wonder how I am actually going to locate her.

Given that I have crossed a replica of the Golden Gate Bridge, it is not unreasonable to expect to find a mirror image of San Francisco on the other side. No such luck. I have arrived in an unfamiliar conurbation whose streets are chock-a-block with souls in transit. It is like a heterogeneous Chinatown. As in Chinatown there are fancy phone booths, but all have been vandalized and their directories stolen. To counter this celestial crime wave, armed constables patrol the streets. There are numerous stores selling consumer durables. All (I am relieved to note) accept American Express and Mastercard. So I will be able to purchase provisions. Or I would be if there were any supermarkets. It soon becomes apparent that there are none, nor any restaurants. Obviously the dead have no further need of sustenance. I will have to think and act quickly, or otherwise face defeat and starvation.

'Tell me,' I say to a cop on the beat, 'how would a man like you go about tracing an old friend or an ex-wife?'

'A man like me would go to the Town Hall and fill in the relevant forms,' he replies. 'But you ain't a man like me. So going to the Town Hall would be a waste of time. It could even be dangerous, given that miscegenation is a capital offence in Hades.'

'Even for a positive with protection?' I say, drawing his attention to the golden bough.

'On second thoughts a man like you wouldn't be wasting his time going to the Town Hall after all,' he says. 'Give 'em the name of the person you're looking for, plus the date of death, and in three months you'll have their address. Guaranteed. Assuming they've had a proper burial, that is.'

'Three months,' I protest. 'I can't wait that long.'

'Why not?' he says. 'What's three months when you've got eternity to play with?'

My rumbling stomach provides the answer.

•

If I have no immediate way of tracing my wife, perhaps I can advertise my presence and attract her to me. My one asset is my camera. Providentially I note a vacant attic with a wall of windows, just the place to establish a temporary studio. The owner (on seeing the golden bough) withdraws his objections. Indeed he volunteers to be my first sitter. Word quickly spreads that a proper photographer has set up shop in town. A line forms, all the way from the street, up four flights of stairs, to the threshold of my wooden door (which remains permanently ajar).

Just when the continuous procession of strangers is causing me to despair, my late wife puts her head around the door. A few weeks before her fatal relapse we had attended a formal wedding. My wife wore a strapless red gown that filled me with desire. I could hardly wait to return to Grant and Lombard and strip it off. When she was naked at last I took a series of black and white photographs. It is as if one of those negatives had just walked into the room. I leap across the floor to embrace her.

'Hold your horses, Mr Photographer,' she says. 'I don't want any funny stuff. I just want a portrait. Something nice for Wyatt.'

I am simultaneously distressed and amazed; distressed because the sitter is not my wife after all, amazed that Josie Earp really is her double. Does this mean that one of the great controversies of the Old West has finally been solved? Is the identity of the woman in the 'Kaloma' photograph now beyond question? I have been afforded a unique opportunity to obtain irrefutable evidence. All I need do is ask Josie to reprise that notorious pose. Her immediate response is not verbal. She blushes; that is to say, her cheeks turn white.

'You wouldn't make such a request if you knew my husband,' she says eventually. 'He's a mite possessive. And he has a tendency to forget that we're under a tombstone, not still in it.'

'At least tell me the name of the lucky man who took the original?' I plead. 'Was it Camillus S. Fly?'

'That's for me to know and you to find out,' she replies coquettishly.

My stomach continues to rumble, reminding me of the need for haste. I ask her to look at me and smile, then press the shutter twice. A modest head-and-shoulders is better than nothing.

'The pictures will be ready in twenty-four hours,' I say.

'I'll be here,' she says.

'Before you disappear,' I say, 'tell me one thing: does the name Perera mean anything to you?'

That stops Josie Earp in her tracks. 'Tomorrow,' she says. 'I'll tell you everything tomorrow.'

I work all through the drowsy night, not that 'night' and 'day' have any distinct meaning in Hades. I do my best to conjure up sufficient light from the perpetual gloom. By morning, however, the illumination becomes irrelevant, because I have run out of film and there is no more to be had this side of the grave. Nevertheless, I continue to go through the motions, using my flashgun to give the charade an extra touch of authenticity. Even as I counterfeit new images, my first sitters are already returning for their framed portraits. Needless to say, they leave empty-handed. Josie shows up for hers in the afternoon, by which time I am weak with fatigue and hunger.

'I'm sorry,' I say, 'I've been too busy to do any processing. You'll have to come back again tomorrow.'

'David,' she says, 'it's me.' Black tears flow down her dove-grey cheeks.

Three times I try to embrace her, three times I try to clasp her waist, but each time in vain. She slips through my hands like a wraith, or a dream that melts, dew-like, with the rising of the sun.

'Please stand still,' I say. 'Let me try to kiss you.'

As I close in upon her puckered lips I hesitate for an instant. My wife, knowing why, steps backward.

'My breath,' she whispers. 'I'm sorry but there are market forces even in heaven. Since there is so little demand for dental floss it is not imported, and therefore unobtainable.'

Ashamed, I reach out for her again.

'I knew it was impossible,' she says, 'but I never gave up hope that you would come for me.'

'Shut the door properly,' I say.

The milling throng on the stairs murmurs its protest at the unexpected delay.

'Now take your clothes off,' I say. 'If I cannot touch, at least let me look upon your loveliness.'

She stands before me in nothing but a patina of smoke. Her head is engulfed by a halo of white light. A radiant white triangle sits between her gunmetal thighs. Her belly button looks like a blanched raisin. Her nipples are like pearls. Milky crescents hang beneath each breast, like twin moons in a cloudless sky. Her lips glow as though lit from within. 'Oh Alma,' I say, 'if only I could hold you.'

As I stride across the room to make another attempt, the door flies open.

'Forgive the intrusion,' says the intruder, carefully folding a street plan, 'but I'm on duty and cannot afford the time to wait my turn. Anyway, I'm here on behalf of my wife. She asked me to pick up some prints.' At which point he finally looks up.

Telling him they're not ready is obviously going to be the least of my problems.

'What the hell is going on!' he demands. 'Josie, put on your clothes while I shoot this prick.'

His hat is white, as is his coat. Not to mention his walrus moustache. But he is unmistakable. So this is the promised end.

One night, when I was a sex-crazed adolescent, my mother caught me watching a maid undress in an apartment across the street. 'Carry on with that sort of behaviour,' she advised, 'and you'll find yourself in serious trouble.' She was right. My obsession with my wife's body is going to get me killed. Why couldn't I have asked her important questions about the experience of dying and the practicalities of being dead instead of simply asking her to strip? Oh well, it seems I'm about to get the answers first-hand.

Wyatt Earp flicks back his coat to reveal the butt of his Buntline Special. 'I will do you one favour,' he says. 'I'll make it quick.'

'It's not what it seems,' cries my wife. But I can see that my assassin's momentum won't be stalled by rational explanation. Not even by the golden bough itself.

'I've always had problems with authority,' he snorts, spinning the chamber of his six-gun. 'Besides, I'll only be doing my duty,' he adds. 'Positives and negatives mix at peril of death in my part of town.'

Earp takes aim at a point between my eyes. I feel like a member of the Clanton gang. Except that I'm smarter. And I'm holding a camera. True it isn't loaded, but it has a flash. The big question is: will it charge in time?

'You're going to feel very bad about shooting me when you discover your mistake,' I say, 'so I want you to know that I forgive you in advance.'

Earp spits on the floor and begins to squeeze the trigger.

With nothing to lose I press the shutter.

Blinded, Earp misses me by a mile.

'Quick!' I cry. 'Grab your clothes and run for it.'

We scuttle down the stairs and hit the street running. My wife sprints like an Olympic athlete attired according to the custom of the ancients. The dead, who have already seen too much of everything, do not bat an eyelid. The only thing that moves them is the sight of the golden bough, at which they jump aside, leaving a clear path for our escape. By the time we reach the edge of the bottomless gorge, Wyatt Earp is nowhere to be seen. My wife even has the leisure to dress.

'Once we're on the bridge we'll be safe,' I say. 'No one will be able to follow us across.'

Unfortunately this confident prediction fails to take

into account the ferocious temper and eating habits of
the bridge's guardian. At our approach, triple-headed
Cerberus sniffs the air and all of its mouths begin to
salivate simultaneously. It is a noteworthy creature:
one that would have had the crowds flocking to the
Sutro Baths in the old days. With its athletic build,
hairy pelt, and massive jaws it most resembles an
Irish wolfhound. Out of those terrifying chops comes
tumultuous barking and the vision of three well-oiled
sarcophagi lined with black razor-sharp shredders of
flesh. I show the monstrous hound the golden bough,
but it is even less impressed than Wyatt Earp.

'Your shoes,' screams my wife, 'are they leather?'

'Leather?' I reply. 'They're Timberland. All-terrain.
Got them specially for this expedition. They cost me a
small fortune.'

'You'll have to sacrifice them,' she says.

'I'd rather not,' I say. 'Can't I give it my Gore-tex
waterproof jacket instead? It's approaching the end of
its working life.'

'So will you be if you don't take off your fucking
shoes!' screams my wife.

Cerberus greedily accepts the overgenerous offering, but my footwear only accounts for two sets of its
jaws. Although it has three of them, there is of course
only one stomach, so you'd think it would be satisfied
with what it had already received. You'd be wrong. It
obviously believes it has three stomachs to fill, and

therefore needs the placebo effect of a third full mouth. It turns its horrid black eyes upon me as if deciding where to begin. Instinctively I reach for my Olympus, anticipating the shot of a lifetime, only to recall that it contains nothing but an exposed roll of Tri-X.

'Feed it the camera!' screams my wife.

'My faithful Olympus?' I protest. 'Isn't there anything else?'

'Only you.'

The three-headed monster is indeed advancing upon me with homicidal intent. There's no time even to remove the precious film, only proof of my incredible expedition. Sadly I cast my camera into the gaping maw and hear the terrible crunch as unbreakable teeth destroy metal and glass. Looking back (from the security of the bridge) I see the unspooled film hanging from its jaw like a strip of lasagne.

'So,' I say to my wife, 'what's it like being dead?'

'Do you remember when we went to Chez Panisse and you couldn't eat a thing?' she asks.

'How could I forget?' I reply.

'That's what it's like,' she says.

'Sounds ghastly,' I say.

'It is, at first,' she says. 'But what you have to understand is that we – the dead – have lost our appetites. Permanently. For us, bodily pleasure is a thing of the past. There are compensations, of course. We have infinite time for contemplation.'

'What of the non-thinkers?' I ask. 'Those for whom the life of the mind is no life at all?'

'There's round-the-clock television,' she says, 'and all the latest movies on video.'

'Tell me,' I say, 'supposing I were to remarry in the fullness of time. Would I get to spend eternity with you, or wife number two?'

'Since carnal knowledge is no longer an option, you would have all the time in the world to explore both our minds,' she replies. 'The dead – with the honorable exception of Wyatt Earp – have no truck with jealousy.'

'Sounds a little dull to me,' I say.

'That's because you're still flesh and blood, still a positive,' she says.

'When do you think you'll make the switch back?' I ask.

'Probably when we reach the upper world,' she replies.

'Let's hope you're right,' I say.

'Perhaps we should have brought Josie too,' she adds. 'They say two negatives make a positive.'

The warden at the far end of the bridge is less than welcoming, though at least he doesn't want to eat us. 'Where the fuck do you think you're going?' he demands menacingly. The golden bough soon fixes him.

Back on the bank of dread, where the hard-done-